Is This Love Fur Real?

Victoria Hamel

PB & A Publishing

eBook Edition ISBN- 979-8-9897583-6-4

Paperback ISBN-13: 979-8-9897583-7-1

Contents

Chapter One

♥

Rat-ata-tat!

Mable Weaverton pressed her head into her palm. When she'd moved in with Carolyn last fall, she hadn't realized Carolyn gave private marching band lessons each summer. Mable took a deep breath and sighed. She had to get this project done. She only had two weeks to submit her report. Which would be very doable if only she could hear herself think.

Tap, Tap, Tap, Tap, Tap!

She adjusted her off-brand noise-canceling headphones. Over the last half hour, it had become clear to her that her headphones only offered a hint of noise-canceling. Now she could feel a headache coming on. Mable didn't do well under deadlines, and this wasn't the first time she'd procrastinated on a project, and odds were it wouldn't be the last time either. As someone with an undergraduate degree in psychology, she had the tools to fix this problem, but it was too late for that. She was officially in panic mode.

If she didn't submit the completed project to the nonprofit that had sponsored her study abroad trip by midnight on the eighteenth, then her grant turned into a loan. Mable didn't know how she'd manage another monthly bill. Her jaw clenched. She already had tens of thousands of dollars in loans. Middle school band students would not cause her to miss this deadline. She just needed to find somewhere quiet where she could write and work on the video script.

She took off the headphones and wiped sweat off her ears. Not only was it too loud to concentrate, but it was also too hot. The temperature was ninety degrees for the fifth day in a row, and their apartment didn't have central air. Mable took a sip of her now lukewarm water and checked the time. If she left now, she could go to Common Grounds and get in a couple hours of work before they closed for the evening. Plus, they kept that place nice and cold.

Mable put on a tank top over her sports bra and packed up her computer. She walked through the living room, giving a quick wave to her roommate, Carolyn. She slid her feet into her flip-flops and quickly exited the apartment. The heat in the stairwell was stifling. By the time she exited the building, sweat had soaked the back of her tank top.

What she would give for a quiet room and the air cranked up to high. If she had any money left over from her summer stipend, she'd be checking into a hotel right about now. She had an emergency credit card. She could use that and book a room for a few nights if she were desperate. Better to put more money on the credit card and get that project done than to have a new loan for the next three years. She frowned and her stomach clenched. Had she been stupid not to stay home over summer break and nanny for a family on the North Shore? Her friend Kelly was making a thousand a week taking care of three kids under five. No time for should-have thoughts right now. What she needed to do was focus on her work.

She drove her ancient Toyota Corolla over to Common Grounds and parked. She went into the coffee shop and was greeted by a packed house and a young man playing an acoustic guitar and singing off-key. *Ugh! Open Mic Night, why me!* She made her way through the crowd and up to the counter.

Mable didn't know if she was going to stay, but having spent the last few years working at Jesse's Pub, she couldn't just walk out of a cafe without making a purchase.

"What can I get you?" the barista said loudly.

"Can I get an iced tea?"

"For here or to go?"

"Um," Mable paused and looked out on the cafe's patio. It was still crazy hot outside, but at least outside she could work without hearing struggling musicians. "Make it to go. I'm going out there," she pointed to the patio.

"Gotcha."

A few minutes later, Mable was outside on the patio. Because of the heat and humidity, she was alone, at least until the mosquitoes began biting. Mable swatted a mosquito and accidentally deleted the first two paragraphs of her paper. Then, when she went to undo the deletion, her bracelet caught on her straw, knocking over her iced tea onto her laptop. Thank goodness she'd gotten the to-go cup. Despite that, she jumped up in a panic and used her shirt to wipe off the keyboard before any liquid could destroy the pricey machine, which deleted more of her document. Now she had to figure out how to get those paragraphs out of the cloud.

Mable tried to take a deep breath, but her throat was closing in frustration and her eyes were tearing, which only made her angrier at herself for getting herself into this mess. She really needed to stop telling herself she worked best under pressure.

Her phone rang. She checked the display and saw it was Sean, her boss, and a second cousin by marriage. Mable took a breath and answered the phone.

"Hey Sean! How's married life?"

"It's been the best two weeks of my life."

"You're still in town?"

"Our flight is tomorrow at noon. But there's been a minor hiccup, and I was hoping maybe you could help us out."

Mable felt her skin grow cold. "Is something wrong? What's going on? Is Nicole okay?"

Sean quickly replied, "Yes! Oh gosh, everything is great, it's just—"

Yip!

"Was that a dog? Oh my God, did you guys get a dog?"

Sean chuckled, and Mable could hear Nicole in the background. "Come here, puppy," she said.

"It's been a wild twenty-four hours, Mable. We are now puppy parents."

"No way! How did that happen?" Mable asked.

"You will not believe this. Some guy was trying to bring a puppy on the train as a gift for his girlfriend, but he didn't have a leash or a crate, so the train conductor told him he'd have to go get a crate or a leash and come back, and this jerk set the puppy down and ran off."

"Who does that?"

"Right? The puppy started following the conductor onto the train and he didn't know what to do." Sean said.

"I'm sure they're used to rowdy passengers, not puppies."

"Exactly, another passenger suggested calling Marley Creek Animal Rescue, so the conductor brought her into the train station and left her with the ticketing agent."

"She's a girl!?"

"Mm-hmm, yes she is."

His tone softened, and Mable could picture him talking to his dog.

"Aww, so how did she get from the train station to you two?"

"Ethan was volunteering when the conductor called. He ran over and as soon as he saw her, he called us."

"I didn't even know you and Nicole were looking for a dog."

"Mable, we didn't know we were either, but once we saw Iggy…"

"Iggy? For a girl dog?"

"That's what I said! Did you hear that, Nicole? Mable agrees with me."

"Hey! I don't want to be on your bride's bad side!"

"Anyway, I know this is last minute, and I'm sorry I didn't call you earlier, but we were at the vet all afternoon."

"So, she has all her shots."

"Yes, she's a very healthy four-pound Yorkie mix."

"Aww, that's so cute. I can't wait to meet your new addition!"

"You don't know how happy I am to hear that Mable, because I need a huge favor."

Mable bit the inside of her cheek. "Okay?"

"Can you watch Iggy while we are on our honeymoon? We're desperate. Nicole says there is no way her baby is going to a kennel."

"Um, I would, but the apartment is small, and I don't think Carolyn will go for it."

"Not at your apartment! We need you to come and stay at our place. Do you think you could stay here and dog-sit Iggy?"

"Your place?" Mable grinned from ear to ear. Two weeks in a house, all to herself? All she had to do was feed and let out a cute little dog? Heck, she'd do that for free.

"Yes, do you think you can come over here and watch Iggy while we're gone? There isn't any food in the fridge, but we'll leave some extra cash for groceries, and we've already ordered Iggy's special food to be delivered tomorrow night."

Mable felt cooler than she had all day. Her salvation was at hand. "Of course! I'd be happy to!"

"You're a lifesaver, Mable!"

"Say thanks to Auntie Mable, Iggy!" Nicole said in the background, and Iggy yipped happily.

Mable giggled. "You're welcome, Miss Iggy!"

"Can you be over tomorrow by nine-thirty? The car is coming at ten to take us to the airport."

"I'll see you tomorrow, Sean."

"Thanks again. Did I already tell you that you're a lifesaver?"

Mable chuckled, "Yes, yes you did."

"See in the morning, Mab!"

"Bye!"

Mable ended the call and quickly downed the rest of her iced tea. She did a little shimmy and then made a beeline for her car. She needed to pack!

***

Mable was tired and wired as she drove to Nicole and Sean's house. When she got home from Common Grounds the night before, she'd had a whole fifteen minutes of quiet to outline her paper, and then Carolyn came rolling in with her girlfriend Sadie, and they had loud sex on the other side of the paper-thin wall from where Mable was staring at her laptop.

She had the windows down and the air cranked high. The sky looked hazy as she drove past the lake on her way to Nicole's. Mable popped in an old One Direction CD and began singing with the boys. She laughed. Leave it to Sean to save her again. Ever since he'd been in her life, he'd had this uncanny way of accidentally fixing her problems.

By the last chorus of one of her favorite songs, she was pulling into Nicole's driveway and turning off her car. She grabbed her duffle bag and the tote bag with her laptop, and walked up to the front door. Before she could press the doorbell, she heard Iggy scratching at the door and barking little barks. She couldn't wait to meet Sean and Nicole's bundle of joy.

Mable pressed the doorbell and waited on the doorstep. She'd only been here once, for a backyard barbecue back in June, and she recalled loving Nicole's back deck. Now it was Sean's as well.

The door swung wide open, and Sean said, "C'mon in!" He was holding the tiny dog in his arms.

She walked in and was quickly enveloped in Nicole's embrace. "Mable, I can't thank you enough for agreeing to watch Iggy on such short notice."

Mable gave Nicole a quick squeeze back and said, "We're family! And besides, you didn't even know there was a puppy in your future last week!"

Nicole laughed, "That's true!" Nicole wrapped her arm around Sean's waist. "Now come here and meet Iggy."

Sean lifted one of Iggy's front paws, "Hi Mable, nice to meet you! Did you see I have glossy chestnut hair, just like my mama?"

Nicole elbowed Sean. "You are so silly!" she giggled. "I have to admit, I never saw myself as a fur mom. But now I can't wait to buy all sorts of cute little tartan outfits in Scotland for our tiny terrier."

"You know she's practically a purebred Yorkshire Terrier, as in England, ancestral enemy of Scotland." Sean said.

Nicole leaned her head on Sean's shoulder and looked down at Iggy in his muscular arms. "I'm going to spend so much money dressing her up! As soon as we get back, we need to figure out her first Halloween costume!"

Mable grinned and shook her head a little. She'd never seen a couple so head over heels for a dog. She reached over and shook Iggy's paw. "Nice to meet you, Iggy. We are going to have a fun couple of weeks until your parents come back."

"Now let's show you around the place," said Sean. He began walking down the hall toward the bedrooms.

After a quick tour of the house and a review of Iggy's toys and eating schedule, Sean and Nicole were getting into their ride to the airport.

Mable held Iggy in her arms and stood on the porch, waving goodbye to the newlyweds. "Bye! Have a wonderful trip! Don't worry about us! We'll be fine!" Iggy squirmed as they waited for Sean and Nicole to stop waving goodbye. Once they were gone,

Mable turned and opened the door to go back inside. As she was juggling the fidgeting dog, Iggy nipped her thumb.

"Ouch!" Mable said. The shock caused her to almost drop Iggy. "What the heck!" she said, and she set the dog down. Iggy promptly ran down the hall. Mable looked at her thumb, surprised to see it was bleeding. Those little puppy teeth were sharper than she thought. Mable sighed and went to the sink to run water over her thumb. *I hope this isn't a sign of things to come. This is supposed to be an easy gig.*

Chapter Two

♥

Ethan poured himself a second keto-friendly margarita and returned to his pool float. He was free of manny duties for the next couple of weeks and he was enjoying the quiet. Not that he didn't love the stuffing out of his charges, Liam and Franklin, but as everyone in Marley Creek knew, the just turned five-year-old twins were full of never-ending energy. Being twenty-three, he still had the energy of youth on his side, but the boys were giving him a run for his money. He pushed a hand through his shaggy, wavy brown hair. When he started working for Devin and Ben, he'd had a buzz cut. Over the last few months, he hadn't gotten around to another haircut, and now it was almost down to his collar.

He pulled up his yacht rock playlist and hit play. The opening chords of the Doobie Brothers began playing, and he hit skip. That song used to be one of his favorites until Becca had ruined it for him. He wasn't ready to recover the song. He hoped someday he'd be able to listen to "What a Fool Believes" and not think about her. Ethan ground his teeth, frustrated that he was letting her spoil his afternoon in the sun.

Summer was his favorite time of year. No matter how hot it got, he loved being outdoors. Lucky for him, Franklin and Liam loved playing outside, so he'd spent more time in the sun this year than he had since he was a lifeguard in high school. He'd applied sunscreen, but all the hours in the sun this summer had left him with a tan. Ethan breathed in the chorine scent of the pool, and that also made him think of Becca and the way she'd crinkle her nose when he'd go over to her dorm room after doing laps at the pool. She'd hated so many things about him. He had no idea why they'd been together as long as they had.

He pushed himself to the edge of the pool. Once again, Becca was ruining his day. Shoot, he was really missing the boys now. Since February, he'd been so consumed with watching the boys that he hadn't had space to think about Becca. Now that he had time to himself, it was back to Becca, Becca, Becca. He knew he should probably contact his therapist.

Unease built up in his body, making his breathing shallow. Ethan felt like a failure and needed a distraction. He sat on the side of the pool and hung his feet over the edge. He unlocked his phone and texted Jax. Jax was always up to hang out. They could go to the gym or, if Jax was working, Ethan could go over to Hop's Heaven and have a beer. Three dots bubbled on his phone, and he waited. The cloud covering the sun had passed over, and now the backyard was flooded with light.

> **JAX: Sorry, me and the GF are camping right now.**

Ethan sighed. *Well, now what? Might as well go to the gym.*

> **ETHAN: Have a good time, avoid bears. LOL**

JAX: LOL (bear waving gif)

Ethan got out of the pool, toweled dry, and went into the house to change clothes and grab his gym bag. When he stepped outside, a breeze ruffled his hair. The humidity of the day had lessened, but it was still hot. He'd always been a slow runner, and he preferred weight training to cardio, but there was something about a late summer afternoon that made him want to run a few miles.

He turned and went back into the house. Once he had armed himself with a bottle of water, he locked the door behind him and did a few stretches in the driveway, and set off toward town. It was about a mile and a half to get from The Belmont's house to Marley Creek's downtown. He planned to run down Main Street and circle back. The run should wear him out enough that he could sleep tonight and keep his mind off Becca. He grimaced. This was his well-deserved vacation. Now here he was letting her slip back into his mind and make him feel like shit. He shook his head. He was going to have to call his therapist, maybe even go back on meds if he couldn't get a handle on his thoughts. His stomach twisted. Ethan would not go back to the dark place he had spent December in.

Before he knew it, he was jogging down Main Street. He passed over the train tracks. On the outskirts of the commuter parking lot, there was a small splash pad. A sprinkling of kids ranging from toddlers to elementary school-aged were running through the dancing water while their parents looked on. *In a couple of years, those kids could be in my classroom.* He inhaled the smell of chlorine mingled with freshly cut grass. All he needed to do was finish two years of college and hope that Ida

B. Wells Elementary had an opening. Or maybe he'd find a job in a surrounding town. One thing was for sure, he wouldn't be going back to Michigan, even if Becca wasn't there. The memories were too much.

Ethan drank the last of his water just as he was nearing Jesse's Pub. He didn't know if there were any water fountains he could hit on the way home, and he hadn't thought to bring a few bucks with him for a drink. Hopefully, Lucas wouldn't mind if he stopped to get some water. He paused his playlist and walked around to the back gate of Jesse's Pub.

The raised garden beds were overflowing with fresh vegetables and herbs. Ethan absently pinched a mint leaf off a plant and rubbed it between his fingers. He popped it into his mouth and chewed. He knocked on the back door of the restaurant and hoped Lucas would hear him over the noise of the kitchen. There was no way he was going to take his smelly, sweaty ass inside the restaurant to ask for a glass of water, even if the owner was his half-brother. Sean would kill him. Just as he was about to knock on the door again, the door burst open.

"Ethan! What the heck are you doing here?"

"Any chance you can refill my water bottle? I'm parched."

"You're parched." Lucas crossed his arms.

"Did Sean tell you to check up on me?"

"Oh God, no! You know Sean wouldn't send me to check on you."

Lucas squinted his light brown eyes and took Ethan's water bottle. He was wearing a Jesse's Pub baseball hat on backwards over his strawberry blonde hair. "I'll be right back." He shut the door and left Ethan standing in the garden.

A minute passed, and then another. Ethan tapped his foot. Had Lucas forgotten about him? Ethan felt his hamstrings tightening, so he bent down and started stretching. He stood and ran a hand through his sweat-soaked hair. Then he felt a pinprick on his thigh. He looked down and swatted a mosquito. A few seconds later, he felt another prick on his upper arm. He smacked his arm and splattered his own blood. He took the hem of his shirt and wiped off his arm.

Bang!

The door flew open. Lucas had his phone up to his ear, and Ethan's water bottle was nowhere to be found.

"Dude!" Ethan said. "About time you came back, I'm getting eaten alive out here!"

"Shh," Lucas said, then, "No, I'm talking to Ethan, not you!" He held up one finger.

Ethan crossed his arms, regretting his decision to stop. He could have been back at the Belmont's in the time it was taking to get a drink.

"It can't be that bad, Mable! Wait, a whole pillow? Do you think she ate any of it?"

Ethan started to get a bad feeling.

"Have you tried bacon?"

The hair stood up on Ethan's arms.

"What do you mean they said not to feed her people food?"

Ethan groaned. "Give me the phone." Ethan held out his hand.

"Ethan wants to talk to you." He handed him the phone.

"Don't do that, I can figure this out!" Mable said into Ethan's ear.

"Erm, it's me."

"Oh hi, Ethan. How's it going?"

"I was out running, and I stopped by Jesse's to get a drink—and what's going on with Iggy?"

"She won't come out from under their bed."

"Did you try to give her one of her treats?"

Mable snorted, "I'm not an idiot."

"Right, sorry about that. So she doesn't like the treats, huh?"

Lucas gestured to Ethan, holding up one finger, and then went back inside. Ethan leaned up against the raised bed closest to him.

"Did I hear Iggy tore up a pillow?"

Mable sighed. "Yes, I'd just gotten set up and was about to work on my paper. I went back into the living room and there was stuffing all over, so of course I ran over and picked up Iggy. I tried to open her mouth, but she squirmed out of my hands and ran under the bed! I've tried everything to get her out, but she won't come to me," her voice rose to a crescendo of panic.

"Mable, it's going to be okay. I'm coming over."

"No, you don't need to do that! I'm sure I'll figure this out!"

"I have nothing better to do. I'm coming over."

"Are you sure?"

"Yes, I feel kind of responsible. I'm the one who told Sean and Nicole about Iggy."

The back door opened, and Lucas walked out holding Ethan's water bottle.

Mable breathed a sigh of relief, "Thank you so much, you're literally a lifesaver!"

"Well, I haven't done anything yet. See you soon."

Ethan disconnected the call. He handed Lucas back the phone and took his water bottle. He popped the top and took a long drink.

"So you're heading over to Nicole and Sean's?" Lucas asked.

"Yep. Keep your fingers crossed that puppy didn't eat any stuffing."

"Will do. Sean was here for a couple of hours yesterday, and he could not stop talking about that dog."

"Wait till you see her," Ethan said.

"He had videos on his phone. The entire staff got to see her."

Ethan grinned. "I knew Sean and Nicole were the perfect parents for Iggy."

"I've got to run. Good to see you, buddy. Let's get together for a beer soon!" Lucas said.

"Sounds great!"

Lucas turned around and went back into Jesse's, and Ethan took the shortcut over to Nicole's house.

Chapter Three

♥

Great, now Ethan had to come over and bail her out. She didn't know him very well, but she'd heard Devin call him the kid whisperer. She hoped he was great with puppies too. Her stomach roiled. If something happened to Iggy, Sean and Nicole would never forgive her. She didn't know if she'd be able to forgive herself. How was she going to be an elementary school psychologist if she couldn't even dog-sit for one day without a disaster?

She walked away from the bedroom and went into the living room; she got on her hands and knees, looking under the couch and chairs for any errant pieces of fluff that Iggy could get her paws on. Mable sat up and leaned back on her haunches. She gathered her long blonde hair and then took the scrunchy off her wrist and pulled her hair through it until she had a topknot. She fanned herself with a magazine that was sitting on Nicole's coffee table. Why was she so hot? It must be her panic.

Knock, Knock, Knock.

Mable hopped up; Ethan was here! She rushed to the door and opened it. Ethan stood on the doorstep. He was wearing a sweat-soaked tank top, and she noticed how it clung to his pecs and his abs down to his tapered waist. She hadn't seen Ethan since Sean and Nicole's wedding. She thought he was cuter since he stopped bleaching his hair and sporting a buzz cut. Now his hair was its natural brown color. It was wet and lying flat, but around his ears it was curly. Sean had mentioned Ethan was big into working out, but she had no idea how fit he was. Mable had the sudden urge to lean over and lick a bead of sweat that was running down his neck and into the hollow of his collarbone. What was wrong with her? Now was not a good time to be attracted to someone!

Mable's face flushed. "I feel terrible asking you to come over." She opened the door and Ethan walked in.

"Pretty sure you didn't ask me to. I insisted I was coming over." He smiled.

Mable liked the way his entire face lit up when he smiled. "But I interrupted your run."

Ethan waved away her apology. "I was literally less than a block away. I thought about running home to change, but it didn't make sense when I was right here. Plus, if Iggy ate something, we need to take care of it."

Mable relaxed her shoulders. Ethan's competency was instantly calming. He knelt and untied his shoes, and then he stood back up and toed them off.

"I'm surprised Iggy didn't come running when you knocked on the door."

Ethan frowned. "That is surprising. What room is she in?" He started walking down the hallway as she answered.

"She's under their bed."

"Crap, it's probably a king-size bed. Well, we are going to have to lure her out. Can you check the refrigerator for cheese?"

"On it," she said, feeling like she was the assistant to a doctor.

She watched him hustle down the hall and admired his mid-thigh shorts. Thank God he didn't wear those baggy mid-calf shorts so many guys wore. She was a girl who liked thick thighs. Ethan might not be very tall, but damn, he looked good in shorts. She shook her head. "Get it together, Mable," she hissed out loud.

Mable opened the refrigerator and groaned as the cool air hit her. Why was it so hot in here? Maybe it was just her. She'd have to remember to ask Ethan if he thought it was hot in the house before he left. Aside from a door filled with all sorts of condiments from brown mustard to gochujang sauce and a few cans of seltzer water, the refrigerator was empty. She took out a can of seltzer water, popped the can open, and took a long drink. Now she felt better. She must have been dehydrated. She placed the can on the counter and walked down the hall to Sean and Nicole's bedroom.

Once inside the bedroom, she didn't see Ethan anywhere. Could he have gone to the wrong room? She turned to leave the bedroom and go to the spare bedroom when she heard Ethan talking.

"It's okay, Iggy. You can come out. I'm not going to hurt you."

Mable walked back into the room and around to the far side of the bed. Most of Ethan's body stuck out from underneath. A warm flush broke out on Mable's chest as she admired Ethan's ass.

She squatted down next to the bed, and he slid out from under it.

He sat up. "Did you find a piece of cheese?"

"The fridge is like totally bare."

"Shoot, okay, is there a squeaky toy? Do you know if there is a toy she likes?"

Mable cheeks reddened, "I don't know. We didn't have a chance to play. If I'm being honest, I don't think Iggy likes me." She looked down.

Ethan rubbed her shoulder. "I'm sure that isn't the case. Iggy is probably just a little scared and confused. She's gone through a lot of change in a very short amount of time."

"I'm positive they got her toys. I just don't know where they are. Let me look at the instructions they left me."

"Sounds good."

Mable got up and went back to the kitchen and picked up the sheet of paper Nicole had written out. She scanned the page until she found what she needed.

"Iggy's toys are in a basket on top of the washing machine."

Now if she only knew where the laundry room was. She walked back to where Ethan was sitting next to the bed. "Do you know where the washing machine is?"

"It's a stackable unit, closet next to the bathroom. The one with the folding doors."

"Awesome! I'll be right back."

Mable walked down the hall and opened the accordion doors. There, on top of the washing machine, was a small pile of dog toys. She picked up a little Yoda squeaky toy and went back to the bedroom. She handed Yoda to Ethan like a scrub nurse giving a scalpel to a surgeon.

Ethan got down on his stomach and looked under the bed, "I think Iggy fell asleep."

"Is that bad?!"

"It's better than if she were throwing up."

"Okay, cool."

Ethan squeezed the toy, and it squeaked. A second later, Iggy barked.

Ethan slowly backed away from the bed, squeezing the toy so that it squeaked, "Come on out, puppy, let's see how you are doing."

Iggy ran out from under the bed and climbed into Ethan's lap.

Mable felt cool relief flood through her. Iggy looked like she was fine.

Ethan began petting Iggy, but she nipped at his hand. "Hmm," Ethan said.

Mable felt the hairs on her neck stand up. "Oh no, does that mean she ate some of the stuffing?"

"Not necessarily. She's not vomiting, retching, or grunting like she's in pain. And she's clearly not lethargic."

"Okay, so we shouldn't worry?" Mable said.

"I don't think so."

"But you can't be sure. Maybe we should call Vet 911?"

"We could try, but it's a Sunday, and they'd probably tell us to watch Iggy and see if she seemed distressed or if she threw up or tried to throw up," Ethan said.

Mable wrapped her arms around herself and plopped down on the bed. "I'm going to have to stay up all night watching her. What if something happens? What do I do?"

Ethan's brown eyes softened as he looked at her. He rubbed his eyebrows and said, "I don't have anything going on. Do you need me to stay?"

Mable covered her mouth, "Would you? No, I can't make you do that." She paused. "It's fine. I can handle it."

Ethan cocked his head and looked at Mable. "It's not a problem at all. I really should stay. If you weren't watching Iggy, Sean probably would have asked me."

Mable frowned, "You know, that is a good point. Why didn't they ask you to watch Iggy? You're good with kids and dogs, right?"

"I mean, I don't want to brag, but—"

"Feel free to humble brag. We all know how you reformed Franklin and Liam," Mable said.

"I wouldn't say reformed. They aren't hardened criminals, they're five."

"Right, sorry, I was totally being ridiculous there."

"Back to Iggy." Ethan leaned over and petted between the tiny dog's eyes. "How are you feeling, girl?" He whispered. Iggy jumped up and made a circle. Then she ran out of the room.

"Where is she going?"

"Not sure. Let's find out."

Ethan left the room, and Mable followed him. Much to her surprise, Iggy ran to the back door and began scratching at it.

Ethan turned back and looked at Mable. "When was the last time she went outside?"

"Um," Mable said, as her ears turned bright red. She adjusted the scrunchie in her hair. "She hasn't?"

"Oh my gosh." Ethan pushed open the back door and followed Iggy outside. He shook his head.

"I'm sorry!" Mable said. "I was distracted. Then the pillow happened, and she ran under the bed."

Ethan turned around and squinted at her. "Have you had a dog?"

"No," Mable said slowly, "But I have four younger brothers and I had to help potty train three of them, so it's kind of the same thing."

Ethan chuckled. "No, no, it's not."

Mable stared at her bare feet on the deck. Ethan had walked down the two steps into the backyard, and she could tell he was trying to stay relatively close to Iggy as she decided where to do her business.

"She's so small, even though the yard is fenced in, I think she could get under the fence if she wanted to, so you're going to have to make sure that you are always outside when she needs to go, or make sure she is on a leash."

"Got it," Mable nodded.

Once Iggy finished going, which took longer than Mable would have guessed, based on her size, Iggy ran around the yard back and forth, yipping and barking at everything.

"Why is she so hyper? Does that mean she ate part of the pillow?"

Ethan waved his hands. "Gosh no, I think she just has the zoomies."

Mable scrunched up her nose. "Zoomies?"

"Yes, sometimes dogs, especially puppies, need to work off excess energy, so they run around and around until they get that energy out."

Mable wiped her hand across her forehead. "Thank goodness!"

Ethan gave Mable a long look, then he looked back at Iggy, who was chewing on a piece of grass. "You know what? I should definitely stay."

"Is it that bad?"

Ethan moved closer and put a hand on Mable's forearm. She absorbed the heat of his touch, and it made her knees weak. "I'm not super worried about Iggy's having eaten something she shouldn't have, but given that you don't have any experience with dogs, especially not puppies, I just think—"

She interrupted him as relief flooded her. "Yes, please stay. I don't know what I'm doing."

Chapter Four

Ethan scratched another mosquito bite on his arm. Iggy was still doing zoomies around the yard. Mable stood on the patio, fidgeting with her hair. She pulled out her scrunchie, and Ethan watched as her long blonde hair fell, first to her shoulders and then down her back. It almost reached her waist. She pushed some errant strands back behind her ear. Ethan's mouth went dry. She looked more beautiful every time he saw her. And now he was spending the night here.

Of course, their attention would be fully focused on making sure Iggy was okay. If anything happened to Iggy, he didn't think he could ever forgive himself. He pulled his slowly drying shirt away from himself. He was glad they were outside right now because he could only imagine how bad he smelled to Mable. If he'd known his quick stop was going to turn into an overnighter, he would have gone back home first and changed. He didn't even have his phone charger.

The sky darkened as the sunset faded into night. Ethan smiled as he watched the lightning bugs wink on and off. He loved this moment, the gloaming, when the last bit of daylight faded away.

He heard Mable sigh.

"Everyone okay?"

"Yeah, it's just been a long day. I thought coming here would make it easy to work on the project I have due." She plopped down on a patio chair and hung her head.

Ethan noticed the way her hair moved forward, covering her face. He wanted to walk over and push the hair out of her face, tilt her head up and tell her how amazing she was. "How's school going?"

"All I need to do is complete a project, including a video presentation, by August eighteenth."

"You've got this."

"Ha! Every time I sit down to work on it, some sort of disaster happens. First, I couldn't concentrate because my roommate was giving private music lessons to fifth graders, and now watching Iggy has turned out to be way more than I thought it would be." She pushed back her hair and looked at Ethan. Her brown eyes were filled with tears, and she blinked quickly.

Ethan walked over and sat down in the chair next to Mable. He put a hand on her forearm. "How can I help?"

Mable wiped her eyes with the back of her hand. "You're already doing more than enough. I'm sorry. I think I'm just overtired. I barely got any sleep last night, and then I was up early to get over here."

"How about this: we'll get Iggy back in the house, try to feed her a little food, and then you go work on your project while I keep an eye on Iggy."

"I can't expect you to do that."

"You don't have to expect it; I'm offering." Ethan's chest tightened. He hoped she'd let him help her. He hated to see her tears.

Mable took a big, shuddering breath. "I'm really not this weepy. I'm just tired and hungry."

"There were days this spring when me, Franklin, and Liam were all crying at the same time."

"No, you're kidding."

"You got me. I didn't actually cry, but my eyes were misty. Life can be hard."

She reached over and brushed his forearm. "There was a mosquito."

Ethan rolled his eyes. "They are eating me alive tonight."

Iggy trotted up the steps and stopped at Ethan's chair. She stood on her hind legs and pawed at Ethan's leg. He picked her up and placed her on his lap.

Mable looked on. "She really likes you."

Ethan gave Iggy a rub behind her silky-soft ears. "I'm sure she'll like you too! Maybe she can tell you aren't used to dogs. Who knows? She's just a silly puppy." He looked down at Iggy and then said in a sing-song voice, "Yes, you are, Iggy, just a silly little puppy." She barked and nipped at Ethan's hand.

"I don't know what's worse, her little puppy teeth or the mosquitoes that won't stop trying to suck my blood," he said.

Mable tossed her blonde hair and put her hands on her knees. "If you're staying the night, we might as well go inside. I'm sure you want to take a shower and get cleaned up." Her gaze dropped to his sweat-stained clothes. She started walking toward the door.

"That sounds fantastic." He said and stood up, carrying Iggy in his arms. "I'm sure I smell terrible."

"No, you don't!" Mable said. "You smell like chlorine and coconut."

Ethan did a quick sniff under one arm. "I think you are just being nice."

Mable held up her hand with her thumb and forefinger an inch apart and said, "Only a little."

"I only smell a little, or you are only being a little nice?" He asked.

"Both," she said and winked.

He followed Mable into the house, noticing her long legs. She was wearing a pair of denim cut-offs that hugged her ass. He figured she was about five feet, ten inches; so, five inches taller than him. He'd never dated anyone taller than him. Well, more accurately, he'd dated less than a handful of people in his life, and they all happened to be just about his height or shorter. He realized he didn't even know if Mable was single, and here he was having inappropriate thoughts about her.

Ethan shook his head as if that could clear his mind of Mable. "Let's make sure Iggy has some food, and then I'll go see if Sean has anything I can wear."

They stood in the kitchen. Ethan looked around. "Where's her food bowl?"

"Sean and Nicole said they don't want to leave the food bowl out all the time, so I put it on top of the fridge." Mable reached up. Her top rose, revealing a tiny cluster of stars tattooed on her ribcage. He wanted to kiss each of those stars as he made his way around to her breasts. He moved so that he was on the other side of the island. Ethan shouldn't think about Mable this way, not when she needed his help. He was sure she wouldn't appreciate him getting all horny over her when he was just here to help with the dog.

"Here we go!" Mable put the bowl on the counter and then pulled out the container of puppy food. Inside the container was a small scoop.

"She's eaten already today, right?"

"Yes, twice." Mable said.

"Okay then, just give her a tiny bit."

"Gotcha, let's do just a tablespoon."

The small pellets tinkled as they landed in the metal feeding dish. Iggy perked up and ran over to Mable. She got on her hind legs and pawed at Mable's calves.

Ethan chuckled as Mable jumped, surprised.

Mable set the bowl on the floor, and Iggy thrust her head into the bowl. She took a bite and began to chew. Then she went back into the bowl and took out a piece of food and ran into the living room.

"What's going on? Is that normal?" Mable rushed after Iggy.

Ethan was quick to reassure her. "Lots of dogs do it. It's fine."

Mable put a hand to her chest, "Thank goodness you are here, or I'd be freaking out right now."

Ethan smiled widely. "You'll get the hang of this in no time."

"I feel like by the time I get it together, Sean and Nicole will be back."

"By the time they get back, you'll be so good at dog watching, they'll probably ask you to come over a couple of times a week to dog-sit Iggy. You'll probably wind up opening a pet psychology practice and doing a podcast on how to communicate effectively with your dog."

Mable snort-laughed, and Ethan felt his heart sing; even her snort was the cutest thing he'd ever heard.

"I highly doubt that. People think it sounds bonkers, but I love working with kids," Mable said.

"Why would that sound bonkers?"

"Well, I spent most of my teen years helping take care of my younger brothers and sister, so you'd think the last thing I'd want for a career is to work with children."

"Our teen years sound similar, except you watched your siblings, and I watched kids in my neighborhood."

Mable cocked her head. "I hadn't realized that." She was really looking at him now, her brown eyes trained on his face as he spoke.

"I always wanted to be a teacher, or Doctor Doolittle," Ethan grinned.

Iggy ran back out of the living room, and they heard her lapping up water.

"She seems to be doing pretty good. I'll go rummage in Sean's closet and see if I can find anything that might fit me," Ethan said.

Mable put a finger to her lips. "Sean's a big guy. What is he, six feet tall?"

"I think he's like six-two. When I was a kid, I thought someday I'd be tall like him, but he must have gotten his height from his mom's side of the family, because our dad is about as tall as me."

"Go figure." Mable said, and then she added, "Who cares about height, anyway."

Warmth flooded his chest, "Exactly, who cares."

Chapter Five

Mable heard the shower running and some music playing. She didn't recognize the song. She wondered if she should get ready for bed as well. Speaking of bed, where would Ethan sleep? Sean and Nicole's house had three bedrooms, but one was currently an office and had no bed. When Sean and Nicole had shown her around the house, she'd put her stuff in the guest bedroom. But now that Ethan was here as well, one of them should take the main bedroom. She couldn't really ask Ethan to sleep on the couch when he was staying here as a favor to her.

She sat on the couch in the living room and braided her hair. If anyone was going to sleep on the couch, it should be her. Iggy was curled up on the kitchen floor, asleep. She wondered if puppies slept through the night or if they were like babies. She should have done some research on dogs and, more specifically, puppies, before she'd shown up here today to watch Iggy for two weeks. Mable really thought this was going to be a piece of cake. The joke was on her.

Mable felt her phone vibrate. She swiped it open and saw a text from Hannah:

HANNAH: Were you able to get hold of Ethan?

MABLE: Yep, there was no way I was going to call Sean and Nicole. I called Lucas at Jesse's. Can you believe while I was on the phone with Lucas, Ethan showed up there?

HANNAH: No way, that's like some cosmic intervention. I'll ask Zaina what it means.

MABLE: I think it means we live in a small town, and everyone is always showing up in everyone else's lives.

HANNAH: This goes beyond small-town chance meetings. He's a cutie too. Maybe y'all will have a summer fling.

MABLE: Even if I wanted to, I have no time! I need to get this project done, and besides, I doubt I'm his type.

HANNAH: Oh please, you're funny and kind and you have all that gorgeous blond hair and those long legs!

MABLE: You're the sweetest.

HANNAH: So, what happened? Is Iggy OK?

MABLE: I think so. We are observing her tonight, and if she seems sick or distressed, then we'll call the vet, but so far, so good.

HANNAH: WE? OMG, is Ethan staying over?

MABLE: It's nothing like that! He's just helping because he's the one who told Sean about Iggy in the first place.

HANNAH: (gif of an actress saying Okay, Sure)

MABLE: (shrugging emoji)

HANNAH: What's happening now?

MABLE: He's taking a shower.

HANNAH: DUDE!

MABLE: You are so silly! Iggy is trying to drag another pillow off the couch. I've got to go.

HANNAH: (eggplant emoji)

MABLE: (eye roll emoji)

Mable tossed her phone down next to her. She curled up on the couch and closed her eyes. The adrenaline and panic of earlier had worn off, and she was exhausted. She heard a rustling noise coming from under the coffee table.

Mable got up and walked around the coffee table. She reached out to take the small throw pillow away from Iggy. Just before her hand could grab onto a tassel and take it away from Iggy, she ran under the recliner with the pillow. "Not again," Mable moaned. She got down on her belly and looked under the chair. Even in the low light, she could see Iggy's dark eyes sparkling with mischief. Iggy had dropped the pillow, and Mable quickly grabbed it. This time, Iggy missed when she tried to sink her teeth back into it. Mable took the pillow and walked it down to the washing machine. She yawned. She'd figure out how to clean the napkin-sized pillow tomorrow.

She smiled as she passed the bathroom. She could hear Ethan singing along with Earth, Wind & Fire. Her chest tightened. Thinking about September just made her remember how little time she had to get her project finished, and today was another day wasted. She was completely worn out and couldn't even manage to watch a dog. She walked back over to the couch and flopped down. Mable picked up her phone and scrolled through pictures from her summer trip. Her eyes grew heavy. She closed them for just a moment.

Sometime later, Mable woke up with a start, pushing a throw off her. *Where am I?* Then she remembered she was at Sean and Nicole's house dog-sitting. And Ethan was here, too. She looked at her smartwatch, but the battery had run out at some point. The living room was pitch black; it must be the middle of the night. How embarrassing! She'd conked out without even saying thank you and good night to Ethan. She felt her face heat. He must have come out and put the throw over her.

Mable turned on her phone's flashlight and walked down the hall to her bedroom. Her bed was empty. She put her phone on the charger and tip-toed down the hall. The door to the main bedroom was ajar. She slowly pushed it open, and she could make out Ethan's form in the bed. For a moment, she stood in the doorway, then she heard the tinkle of Iggy's collar. Iggy was the little spoon to Ethan. Mable watched for a moment as Iggy made little growling noises and moved her little paws like she was running in a dream. She slowly backed out of the doorway and pulled the door shut behind her.

Thank goodness Ethan was here.

She went back to the guest bedroom and pulled out a pair of sleep shorts and a tank top, then went to the bathroom to change and brush her teeth. A few minutes later, she was tucked into bed. She checked the time. It was three thirty-three. She smiled. It always felt like good luck was headed her way when she checked the time and it was all the same number.

Chapter Six

♥

He was in the emergency room, and a doctor was telling him that there was no cure for his illness. His heart had been broken, and they were going to need to take some blood to see if it could be repaired or if he was dying. He felt pain as a nurse, who also looked just like Mable, jabbed him with a needle. Then the doctor, who was Liam, started barking at him. Ethan jerked awake and rolled away from Iggy. He swung his legs over the side of the bed, his dream still lingering as he rubbed the spot where Iggy had nipped him.

"Let me guess, bathroom time?"

Yip!

Ethan stood and stretched. Iggy was a smart cookie. She was going to give them a run for their money for the next two weeks. Ethan rubbed his face. Mable could probably handle it from here, and he could go home and do what? He'd gotten so used to taking care of the twins, he'd forgotten how to just do what he wanted to do. Iggy ran around his legs and then to the back door and pawed at it, then back over to him, and she pawed him.

"I'm coming, I'm coming." He walked down the hall and noticed the guest bedroom door was open. He looked in and saw Mable fast asleep. According to his smartwatch, it was only seven-thirty. Ethan was used to being up with the twins by six a.m., but he assumed Mable probably stayed up later and slept in much later than the twins. He felt a pang in his chest. Boy, did he miss those wild boys. He couldn't wait to see their faces when they came back and got a chance to meet Iggy. More than likely, the boys would soon beg their parents to get them a dog. Ethan made a mental note to do a little research to make sure he was up to date on which dog breeds were good with high-energy kindergarteners.

Ethan slid into a pair of Crocs that must have been Sean's because they were huge, and he let Iggy out into the yard to do her business. She trotted out into the yard and quickly peed. Instead of coming back to him, she pranced out to a flower bed and began barking at some bright pink zinnias. Ethan watched to make sure she didn't eat any of the flowers. He could really go for a cup of coffee right now. He sat down on a chaise lounge and tried to be in the moment.

Since he'd climbed out of his depression, he'd been going, going, going. This was the first time he'd found himself at loose ends. He had no responsibilities and no plans until the Belmonts came back. He leaned back and propped his feet up. It was time to let himself relax. He listened to the hum of the cicadas and watched Iggy dig a hole in the garden bed.

"No, Iggy, no don't do that, He patted his leg. Come on, Iggster, time to come inside and have breakfast."

Iggy ignored him and kept digging. Ethan sighed and wished he'd thought of bringing out a treat or a squeaky toy, in case he needed to lure Iggy back in. This was something else he needed to tell Mable she should do. He got up and walked over to Iggy. "One last chance. Stop digging. Let's go back into the house."

He crossed his arms. Iggy kept digging, so he bent down and picked her up, and carried her into the house. "You need a bath," he said.

"Well, that's pretty rude," Mable said. She playfully stuck her tongue out at him.

Ethan chuckled and held up Iggy. "She was out in the flowerbed digging."

"That's probably not good, right?"

"The important thing is that she is feeling fine, so we know she didn't eat any of the pillow stuffing."

"That is a huge relief. I would feel awful if anything happened to her on my watch."

"You and me both," he said. "But no, it's not great. No one likes to have their dog digging holes in the yard. Plus, if she is digging holes, she could dig one and squeeze her little butt under the fence and that would be—"

"A nightmare!"

"Exactly," he said.

"What should I do?"

"Never leave her outside alone. When Sean and Nicole come back, they can figure out how they want to handle it."

"So now what?"

Ethan cocked his head. Have you ever given a dog a bath?

No, but I've given all my brothers a bath.

"It's basically the same thing, but more hair."

Mable did her snort laugh and Ethan wanted to give himself a high five for getting her to make that sound again. It tickled him to no end.

Once they finished laughing, she looked at him shyly and asked, "Do you need to head out or can you assist with the bath?"

"I have nothing going on. Let me see what kind of shampoo they have." Ethan handed Iggy to Mable. "Take her into the bathroom, and I'll check for shampoo and get some towels."

Mable went into the bathroom and shut the door. "Look at you, Miss Iggy. You're a mess."

Ethan opened the linen closet. He pulled out a basket that was filled with body wash and lotion. He pushed that basket back and then pulled out another one. In this basket were a few bath toys, a licking mat to suction to the wall, and dog shampoo. Ethan took the shampoo out and walked over to the bathroom. He knocked on the door. "Do you have her?"

"Yep!"

He pushed open the door. Mable was sitting on the side of the tub. Iggy was in the enormous bathtub, trying unsuccessfully to climb out. "That was a great idea, Mable."

Mable smiled, "Thanks. I hope I'm getting the hang of this."

"The bathtub is so big, we'd better give her a little bath in the sink. Sound good?" Ethan said.

"Her hair is so long; we should probably use some conditioner too," Mable said.

Ethan held up the bottle. "We're in luck. They've got a two-in-one shampoo and conditioner."

"Nothing but the best for you, Iggy-poo!" Mable said as if she were talking to a baby.

Ethan guffawed. He filled the sink halfway and stopped to check the water temperature, and picked up Iggy. "I'll hold her, and you lather her up. Does that work for you?"

Mable nodded. "Let's do this." She stood up and walked over to the sink. She put a dollop of the shampoo in her palm and moved close to Ethan.

Ethan could smell Mable over the scent of the shampoo. She smelled like sunflowers. *Of course she did.* He held Iggy as tightly as he could without hurting the puppy. She yipped as Mable began washing her fur. Fortunately, within moments, Iggy relaxed. As Ethan stood there, Mable leaned in, concentrating on her task. Ethan went rigid as she brushed against him, her breasts pressed against his arm. Suddenly, he was very aware he was standing there in an old pair of Sean's shorts and T-shirt, and she was only wearing a tank top and shorts. It felt like it had been years since he was this attracted to anyone. His musings were interrupted as Mable stepped back from his side, suddenly leaving him cold.

"Okay, I think she's good. Let's rinse her off?" Mable said. She wiped her hands on a towel and then pushed down the plunger, releasing the drain.

Iggy barked and tried to scrabble out of Ethan's hands. "It's okay, shh shhh," said Ethan. Mable turned on the water, and Ethan eased Iggy through the stream of water. She barked and tried to bite the water. Mable turned off the water, and Ethan put Iggy on a towel he'd placed on the sink. The moment he let go of her, Iggy shook herself, and water splashed on Ethan and Mable. Mable laughed, and Ethan handed her a hand towel, and he toweled Iggy dry.

Mable looked at the wet dog. "Now we just need a brush."

"I'll be right back!" Ethan ran back to the bucket where he found the shampoo to look for a brush.

He returned to the bathroom and paused at the doorframe, watching Mable rocking Iggy like a baby. Within seconds, Iggy revolted against the rocking and started trying to climb up Mable. Mable threw her head back in frustration, and Ethan wanted to run over and give her a hug. Instead, he said, "I found a brush. Put her down and let's see if we can brush her."

Mable put down Iggy and brushed the wiggly puppy's fur.

"She's so cute! I just want to put ribbons in her fur!" Mable said.

"It's a good thing she is so cute. It really helps you look past all the puppy behaviors," Ethan said.

Mable shook her head. "Just like a kid."

Ethan put Iggy on the floor, and she scurried off. A few seconds later, they heard a toy squeaking.

"Hopefully that will keep her busy for a little while," Ethan said.

"Thank you so much for all your help. I really don't know what I would have done without you last night," Mable said.

"I was happy to help," he responded.

"I'm sure we'll be fine now. I think I've got the hang of things," Mable said. They walked down the hall and into the kitchen. "Would you like a cup of coffee before you go?"

"I could really use some caffeine," Ethan said.

Mable looked at the counters. "Hmm, I don't see a coffeemaker."

"Is it in a cabinet?"

Mable opened and shut various cabinet doors and didn't find a coffeemaker. Then she opened a cabinet that had a few rows of coffee mugs. "I found the mugs."

Ethan walked over and looked in the cabinet. "Look, it's a French press."

Mable pursed her lips. "I've had French press coffee, but I have no clue how to make it."

"Same here."

They stood in silence for a moment and then longer. Ethan felt paralyzed by the awkwardness. Unable to think of anything to say, he cleared his throat. "Well, I better get going." He walked out of the kitchen and over to the front door, where his running clothes sat in a bag next to his shoes.

"I can give you a ride home!" Mable said suddenly.

"No, no, I'm good. I'll stop at Books and Breads on my way home and grab a coffee."

"Are you sure? It's a long walk."

"I'm good," Ethan said.

"If you're sure," she said, trailing off.

Ethan put on his shoes and nodded.

"Well, thanks again," Mable said.

"No problem!" Ethan opened the door to step out.

Mable said, "I can call you later? Let you know how Iggy is doing?"

Ethan felt his heart swell, "I'd like that!" he said over his shoulder, suddenly too shy to make eye contact with her. Then he walked out into the day.

Chapter Seven

♥

Mable double-checked Sean and Nicole's kitchen and pantry, hoping they might have an energy drink or two lying around since she had no clue how to use the French press and didn't feel like trying to figure it out. After an extensive search, she'd found zero energy drinks, and she was getting a headache. She needed to eat and drink something now.

Iggy trotted up to her and nipped at her big toe. She'd forgotten to feed Iggy. *Boy, do I suck at this dog-sitting thing.* She took out Iggy's food and carefully measured the correct amount. By the time she put down the bowl for Iggy to eat, the puppy was literally drooling. "Sorry I took so long, Iggy-bell," she said and petted Iggy's head. Iggy growled and Mable quickly removed her hand. "I'll leave you alone to eat," she said and backed away. She sat on the floor crisscross style and watched Iggy eat. She needed to go get an iced coffee and a donut or something, but she didn't think she should leave Iggy alone. What if she ate something she shouldn't have while Mable was in line at a drive-thru? She hoped Iggy liked car rides.

Mable took a quick shower, braided her wet hair, and put on a pair of shorts, sandals, and a Jesse's Pub T-shirt. She checked her phone just in case Sean and Nicole had tried to call her. Hopefully, they were much too busy enjoying Scotland and each other to even think of calling her. She reread her Iggy care instructions. Turned out Iggy had a little harness to wear that clipped so she could ride in the car without bouncing around. Mable was relieved she wouldn't have to worry about Iggy running around or trying to climb into her lap while she was driving.

Before she tried to put on the harness, Mable walked down the hall and closed the doors to the bedrooms and the bathroom. Her chest expanded with pride, having figured out one way to avoid Iggy running away and hiding from her. She took a training treat and walked over to Iggy. She held out the treat in one hand and, as soon as Iggy gobbled it up, Mable held her with her other hand and got the harness on. However, just as she was about to clip it on, Iggy squirmed free and started running around the living room.

Three tries later, both Iggy and Mable were breathing hard and finally ready to leave the house. Mable went through the drive-thru at The Donut Warehouse and got a large iced coffee with extra cream and a chocolate donut. When she got to the window, Iggy was barking happily and wagging her tail in the back seat.

"What a cute dog!" the teenage employee said.

"Thanks, I'm dog-sitting."

"Can she have a pup cup?"

"What's that?"

"It's a mini cup of whipped cream."

"I better not. She's not supposed to have any people food."

"Aww, bummer," the employee said.

"Thanks, though."

Mable pulled out of the drive-thru and took a long drink of her iced coffee. The caffeine needed to kick in as soon as possible. Chasing Iggy around had used up a chunk of her energy reserves, and today she really needed to get some work done on her project. Her phone buzzed, and she checked the display. A picture of Hannah making a goofy duckface was on her screen. She pulled into a parking space and answered the call.

"Hey there!"

"Where are you at?" Hannah said.

"I'm in the parking lot of The Donut Warehouse, why what's up?"

"I made a little something for you. Can you swing by the shop?" Hannah asked.

"Um, I've got Iggy in the car?"

"No problem, all creatures are welcome at New Age Stones and Witch Crafts."

"You sound like you're reading a commercial."

"Sort of. I was literally reading a sign Zaina has hanging up in the store window."

"Okay, well, if it's cool, then I'll swing by," Mable said.

"I'm so excited to meet Iggy!!"

"Listen, she looks adorable, but she is very naughty!" Mable said the second part in a sing-song voice, aiming her comments at the dog in question.

"Alright, cool, get your butt over here."

"See ya soon!"

Mable checked her watch. It was almost eleven now. She needed to make this stop quickly so she could spend the afternoon working, hopefully without too many Iggy interruptions. It was a short drive to New Age Stones and Witch Crafts, and within a few minutes, Mable was parked and clipping Iggy's leash to her harness.

She was feeling light as she walked into the shop. Maybe she was getting the hang of taking care of Iggy.

Ding dong.

When the door chimed, Hannah looked up from the counter. Her red hair was cut in a shoulder-length bob, and as she saw Mable and Iggy, she smiled, which showed off her one dimple.

"Oh. My. Gosh! She's the cutest dog I've ever seen!" Hannah ran around the counter and reached down to pet Iggy. She put out her hand for Iggy to smell, and Iggy nipped her finger.

"Ouch!" Hannah said. Iggy wheeled back and then got twisted in her leash.

"I'm so sorry! I don't know what to say. Iggy! Why are you trying to bite people?!?"

Hannah took a pump of the hand sanitizer the shop kept on the counter and cleaned off her hands. "It's fine. She didn't break the skin."

"It's my fault. I shouldn't have brought her."

"I practically begged you to bring her." Hannah pushed her glasses back up on her freckled face. "I'll give her space, and I'm sure we'll get along fine."

Iggy barked three times in a row and then started pulling Mable toward the store's reading nook. "Well, this is weird. She hasn't pulled on the leash until now."

"Sometimes Zaina says we have a friendly spirit on staff. Could be Iggy senses our ghost?" Hannah shrugged.

Mable chuckled.

"Can I get you a cup of tea?"

"It's so hot, I can't do tea."

"We have bottled water and some probiotic sparkling water."

"I'll try the sparkling water."

Hannah pulled a can from the mini-fridge and brought it over to Mable. Then she went back over behind the counter and pulled out a spray bottle. "I made you a project spray. And don't worry, it's safe for dogs."

"A project spray?"

"Yes, because I know how stressed you are about the assignment you're working on, so I made a spray. It has rosemary to help you with your concentration and chamomile to reduce anxiety." Hannah took off the top of the spray bottle and did a quick spritz in the air.

Iggy sneezed. Hannah and Mable said, "Aww," in unison.

"She's sweet when she isn't being naughty. My plan today is to tucker her out so she'll take a nice long nap and I can get some work done."

"If I wasn't working, I could help," Hannah said. She pushed her glasses up her nose and sat down across from Mable.

"Thanks for saying that, but she's my responsibility. You're really the best. Thank you so much for this spray."

"You're welcome! Now tell me more about how things went with Ethan. I remember at Sean and Nicole's wedding, when he wasn't chasing around those twins, you two were looking very cozy at your table."

Mable felt heat rising up her neck. "He is cute, no doubt about that, and he is great with Iggy, but I don't know. I'm just not good with dating stuff."

"What's to be good at? You like him, he likes you."

"First of all, I don't know if he likes me, and I said he was cute. I didn't say I liked him." Mable said.

"Do you like him?"

Mable was certain her face was beet red. "I enjoy being around him? I can't say I'm not attracted to him. I mean, he came over and he was wearing a tank top and these running shorts, and his thighs, oh my goodness."

"Then what are you waiting for? He's single. You're extremely single. You have his number now, right? What if you asked him out for coffee?"

"You're killing me! I can't do that. Like I said, I'm bad at the dating thing and nothing good comes out of most relationships. I have two concerns right now: getting the summer abroad project done and making sure Iggy is safe and sound. I can't be asking Ethan out for coffee and whatnot."

"Lot of excuses there. What's really going on?"

Mable looked at her feet. "When I say I'm not good with dating stuff, I really mean it. I didn't date in high school because I was too busy babysitting my siblings."

"Did you go to prom?" Hannah crossed her legs in the chair.

"I did, but I went with a group of girlfriends."

Hannah nodded.

"In college, my total dating life has been literally a handful of dates. And some of those were just hookups that led to oral at best."

"I hope it was mutual." Hannah raised an eyebrow.

"Yes, but honestly, it wasn't very good. I would have been happier to stay home with Rex."

"And Rex is? Some guy you met in Germany this summer that you face-time for pleasure?"

Mable burst out laughing. "I love how unfiltered you are. I'm so glad we met."

Hannah made a heart with her hands. "It's crazy that we've only known each other since like February. I feel like we've been friends for ages."

"Right! Here I am telling you my deepest secrets. You'd think we'd been besties since grade school or something."

Hannah smiled broadly and reached for her tea. "Now back to Rex. Is he someone you met this summer or what?"

Mable leaned down and covered Iggy's ears. "This is so embarrassing! Rex is the name I gave to my trusty ten-mode bullet vibrator."

Hannah almost choked on her tea. "Oh, Mable!" they both laughed so hard that soon they were both gasping for breath.

"I-I thought Rex was some dashing German! I was picturing blonde hair, lederhosen and tanned legs!"

"I wish! I didn't meet any hot guys while I was there! There were only a couple of guys in my cohort, and they weren't single."

"Rex," Hannah said. "It is a good name for a vibrator. You're definitely better off with a Rex than some of the guys I've dated in the past. Especially Garry." Hannah shuddered.

"Garry was the guy you were with before you moved to Marley Creek?" Mable asked.

Hannah nodded. "Mm-hmm, and that's a story for another day, over at least one pitcher of margaritas. But back to you; if the only reason you don't want to see where things could go with Ethan is because you're a virgin, my advice is don't let that stop you."

"Ugh, I hate the word *virgin*."

"Okay, my bad, what should we call it? Waiting for Mr. Right? Lightly experienced? Devoted to Rex?" Hannah's eyes sparkled with silliness behind her glasses.

Mable tilted her head. "Rex on the brain?"

Hannah laughed, "Rex on the beach?"

Mable sighed. "I need to get back to the house and get to work." They both stood up, and Mable unwound the leash that Iggy had gotten tangled around her chair. Once Iggy was free, they started walking toward the door.

"Do you think you'll text Ethan?"

"I don't know. I hate to bother him. He's already given up a whole day just to help with Iggy."

Hannah rolled her eyes. "I'm sure he enjoyed every minute he spent with you."

Mable rolled her eyes back. "Okay Hannah, if you say so."

"You spend all your time studying and working. I think you deserve to have some fun before the summer is over, and who knows, maybe he's Rex-worthy."

"Rex-worthy? What does that even mean?"

"Worthy to take Rex's place."

"Oh," Mable said slowly, and the corners of her lips turned down. She thought about the curl of Ethan's hair and his muscled forearms and the way he never made her feel uncomfortable. "Maybe."

Hannah made a squeaking sound of joy. "I love this for you!"

"Don't get too excited. Who knows what will happen?" Mable said.

"Right, note to self: make a confidence spray for my BFF."

Mable gave Hannah a hug.

"I'll talk to you later."

"If anything happens with Ethan…"

"You'll be the first to know."

Hannah opened the door for Mable, and Iggy ran out, pulling Mable behind her onto the sidewalk.

Chapter Eight

♥

Ethan was lying on the couch watching old episodes of the TV show *Psych* and every time the main character's love interest, Juliet, came on the screen, her long blonde hair and bright smile made him think of Mable. By the fourth episode, he had to admit to himself that he might have a thing for Mable. He had zero interest in anyone since Becca. Becca had wrecked him so thoroughly he didn't think he could be a worthy boyfriend for anyone. Mable deserved someone who wasn't already broken.

Not pursuing his attraction to Mable was the right thing to do. He excelled at being a friend. He could be Mable's friend, and in time, his crush would fade away. Proud of himself for avoiding setting himself up to be smashed to smithereens again, he walked into the kitchen and started to make himself a ham and cheese sandwich. As he took out the last two slices of bread, he saw that one piece had green mold. *Ugh*. He tossed the bread and then used some iceberg lettuce instead. The result was dissatisfying, but he was starving, so he ate his sandwich. He thought about sending a text to Mable and checking in on Iggy. Things were probably fine, but just in case Mable had any dog questions, he could be there for her.

Ethan sent Mable a quick text asking how her day with Iggy was going. His phone was almost dead, so he put it on the charger and went for a swim in the pool. The feeling of not knowing what to do with himself was back, and he still had nearly two weeks before the twins came home. He was tempted to call Devin and see if he could FaceTime the boys.

After a swim in the pool, he sat on a lounge chair to dry and looked around the yard. There must be a project here somewhere. He looked out at the lawn and the bushes. If Devin and Ben didn't already have a great landscaping company, he'd be out there right now, mowing the grass. When he'd lived at home, doing yardwork and later maintaining their car, had been a way to show his mom how she could count on him after his father left.

The smell of grass had become bittersweet for him the year his dad left him and his mom. It was the summer before his seventh grade. He'd been full of hormones kicking around his body. He'd felt so awkward. His hair had suddenly gotten greasy, his underarms stank if he rode his bike or played baseball, and then there was the hair sprouting. That last part he remembered being pretty proud of. And just as he was learning about wet dreams, his dad up and left.

By winter break, they'd moved from their house and rented a condo. Losing a backyard was nothing compared to how he'd lost the mom he'd known his whole life. Ethan took a deep breath and shook his head. What good was ruminating about the past? His mom was doing much better now. He got up and checked his phone to see if Mable had messaged him back. Nothing yet.

He walked into his bedroom and turned on his laptop. He checked his email and saw that he'd gotten a reply from West Chicago University; he clicked it open. They had night classes in elementary education! Ethan wasn't sure if he was ready to resume college. Maybe he should wait a little longer before trying to go back. Then again, he'd be going to a completely different school than he'd gone to back home, and there was no way he'd run into Becca on campus. His cursor hovered over the Make an Appointment button. And then he exited out of the email. He could sleep on it and see how he felt later this week.

Ethan checked his watch. No new texts from anyone. He knew it wasn't healthy to sit around waiting to see if Mable replied to him, especially since they were only possibly friends at best. Getting other ideas into his head could only wind up hurting him in the future. He checked the weather app; it was actually under ninety for the first time in days, so he decided to go for a bike ride into town; that way he could pick up some fresh bread from Donnie's Books and Breads. Maybe he'd get a picture book for the boys while he was there.

Within an hour, he was locking his bike up in front of Donnie's place. A sign on the door said they were having Brownie Book Club next week. Ethan's mouth watered. He loved a good brownie. He should see what book the club was discussing. The door chimed as Ethan walked into the shop.

He breathed in the scent of freshly baked bread and spied the bookcases loaded with books for kids and adults alike.

Donnie was behind the bakery counter filling a box with cookies for an elderly man who was wearing a fedora and leaning on a cane. Donnie stood just under six feet tall. His full head of hair had turned gray years ago, causing some people to assume he was older than his forty-five years. He'd recently grown a beard that had come in salt and pepper.

Ethan gave him a wave and went over to look at a table of new releases. He picked up and put down a couple of thrillers, and then he made his way over to the picture book table and began thumbing through the books. He was looking for a book about going to kindergarten that he could start reading to them when they came home in the week leading up to the start of kindergarten. His heart lurched. Pretty soon, they'd be in school all day, and that would free him up to go back to school and work on completing his teaching degree. He chewed on the inside of his mouth. He knew he needed to push through his discomfort; he knew it was PTSD from last fall, but that didn't help his fight-or-flight mechanism.

"Ethan, buddy!" Donnie cried.

"Thank goodness." Ethan muttered under his breath.

"Hi, Donnie!"

"What are you doing here on this lovely summer evening? You should be hanging out with your buddies or on a date or something."

"Well, I'm here now, Donnie. Are you saying I can't hang out with you?" Ethan cocked an eyebrow.

"You know I'm an old fart. I figured you've got better things to do than hang out with me."

"Don't sell yourself short. You aren't that old."

"Let me tell you, when I'm up at three in the morning getting ready to head over here to bake, I feel every one of my forty-plus years." Donnie cracked his back and lifted his arms above his head. "I'm about ready to close up. Did you just come for bread or a book for the boys, or did you want to hang out and have a beer?"

"A beer sounds great. Whatcha got?"

"One sec." Donnie walked into his kitchen. A moment later, he was back holding a couple of bottles of beer and two frosty glasses.

"What's that?"

Donnie turned the bottle Ethan's way. On the bottle was a picture of a book, and it said Annotated Ale. "It's from Hop's Heaven. Jasper and I did a collaboration." Donnie brought the beers over to a table, and Ethan sat down. Donnie opened the beers and poured one for each of them. "I should say, a collab, I forget the kids like to abbreviate everything."

"Speaking of kids, how is Sebastian?"

"He prefers Bastian. He's going to have his learner's permit soon."

"Dang," Ethan said, and he clinked his glass against Donnie's. They both took a sip of their beers, and then Ethan spoke. "Yesterday I wound up spending the night over at Sean and Nicole's."

"Aren't they on their honeymoon?"

"Yes, long story short, they got a dog, and they asked Mable to dog-sit the puppy."

"Hmm." Donnie stroked his mustache.

"Turns out, Mable's never had a pet dog or watched a dog before, so she had some trouble, and I went over to help."

"And you had to spend the night?" Donnie leaned forward in his chair.

"Ah, I didn't have to, but Mable was pretty stressed out. I would have felt terrible just leaving."

"Did you stay for the dog or the girl?" Donnie's brown eyes bored into Ethan's.

Ethan took a big gulp of his beer and looked at the glass cases filled with sweet and savory breads. "Hey, is that pepperoni bread new?"

"It is. It's a pretzel roll with pepperoni and sharp cheddar. Now, back to Mable."

"Way to put me on the spot, Donnie, Ethan sighed and rubbed his arm. "When you put it that way, honestly, I doubt I would have stayed over if it wasn't Mable and at Sean and Nicole's house."

"You like her."

"I'd be lying if I said I wasn't attracted to her. She has this snort-laugh, and nothing is better than when I can get her laughing." Ethan shrugged. "I don't know. Yes, I like her."

"I think that's great. You should ask her out."

"I don't know. I mean, I'm finally in a good place emotionally. I don't think I'm ready to go back into the dating pool. I literally almost drowned last time."

Donnie walked over to the bakery case. He grabbed a pair of tongs and removed a pepperoni pretzel roll and put it in a toaster oven. "I don't think I understood how it was for you."

"Some of it is just a blur at this point. I didn't get out of bed; I didn't shower; I didn't eat. The pain was so bad, I couldn't imagine a time when it would release its grip on me. I was so angry and miserable. I don't know what would have happened if my friend hadn't texted the university's mental health hotline."

Donnie opened the oven and took out the roll. He put it on a small plate, brought it over to their table, and set it in front of Ethan.

Ethan looked up as Donnie sat down. "You're not going to have one?"

Donnie rubbed his moderately rounded belly. "I'm watching my carbs. I missed having a summer bod this year, but maybe I can have a more svelte autumn."

"Come with me to the gym!" Ethan said.

"The thing about running a bakery is that you really don't have time to hit the gym. I'm here from four a.m. 'til about two, and then I come back most days from five to eight for the book side of the business."

"I don't think I realized how many hours you work; boy, you have no time for a social life."

Donnie twisted his wedding ring. "And it's mostly my doing. Maggie's been gone for ten years, and I still don't think I'm ready."

"Then you must understand where I'm coming from."

"Yes, and no. I know this sounds trite, but you're young and you've got so many years ahead of you."

"And what are you, forty-five? You're only halfway to ninety!"

Donnie laughed, and Ethan joined him.

"Seriously, I know it's scary, but just think about it. Ask yourself if Mable is anything like your ex."

"I'll think about it." Ethan took a big bite of his roll, chewed, and spoke through the food. "This is fantastic!"

"If it does well, I'm thinking of adding an olive and feta roll too," Donnie said.

"Let me know if you need a taster for any of these savory rolls. I'm available anytime." He took another swig of his beer.

Ethan's phone chimed. He quickly pulled it out of his pocket. There was a text from Mable. He swiped it open,

MABLE: Any chance you are free? I could use your Iggy skills.

Ethan typed a reply.

ETHAN: I'll be right over.

MABLE: (phew emoji)

Ethan drank the dregs of his beer and popped the last bite of his roll into his mouth. "I've got to run. Duty calls."

"I thought the twins were out of town."

Ethan waved his hand, "Not them. Iggy. That was a text from Mable. She needs my help."

"I hope everything is okay!" Donnie frowned.

"Most likely it's puppy behavior and no big deal," Ethan said as he rushed out the door.

Chapter Nine

♥

Mable's head was pounding.

Bark! Bark! Bark! Bark!

The sharp sound of Iggy's barks was like having ice picks stabbing her eardrums. She was going to puke. Mable checked her phone. It had been five minutes since Ethan had said he was on his way. She had no clue how long it was going to take him to get to Sean and Nicole's. She hoped he was nearby. Panicked, she tugged on her braid. "It's okay, Iggy, everything is going to be okay," she said through the door. "Uncle Ethan is on the way; he's going to help get you out."

Iggy whined and scratched at the door. Then she resumed her barking. *Yap! Yap! Yap! Yap!*

Mable wondered how long Iggy could yip, yap, and bark. If she had been yelling and crying for the last hour, she'd have lost her voice. She pulled her tank top away from her overheated skin and fanned herself. She was desperate for the barking to stop. Her stomach was in knots. If Ethan didn't get her soon, she was going to have to call the fire department, and that would be absolutely humiliating.

Mable lay down on the floor and spoke over Iggy's yipping. "It's going to be okay Iggy, just please stop barking for a minute!" She slid her fingers under the door to comfort Iggy. But instead of comforting the distressed puppy, Iggy chomped her middle finger.

"Ouch!" she shouted and pulled her hand out from under the door, scraping the knuckles of her fingers. She put her finger in her mouth without thinking and then spit it out as she realized Iggy's saliva was all over it. "Oh my God, gross!" She squealed and ran into the bathroom to rinse her hand with hydrogen peroxide and her mouth with mouthwash. The peroxide washed over her hand across the scrapes left by the door. She took a shuddering breath as the peroxide stung and bubbled over her roughened skin. Tears of exhaustion pricked her eyes. She checked her phone. Only five minutes had passed since the last time she'd looked to see if Ethan had said anything else.

She rinsed her burning hand under cold water. *At least the water was drowning out the sound of Iggy's barking.* Mable blushed and her chest tightened. She shouldn't be having mean thoughts about Iggy. It wasn't the dog's fault she was locked in the guest bedroom. This afternoon had been an epic disaster.

Ding dong!

Mable turned off the water and ran out of the bathroom without even drying her hands. Her hand slipped off the knob as she tried to open the door. "One sec!" she yelled, and she dried her hands on her shorts and tried the door again. Mable opened the door and threw herself into Ethan's arms. "Thank God! You're finally here!"

Ethan stumbled a little, but his muscled arms hugged Mable back. She breathed in the summer smell that was all Ethan and calmed down.

She let go of Ethan except for his hand, and she pulled him into the house. "It's been a nightmare, a total nightmare!" She let go of Ethan's hand.

He slipped off his sandals. "What happened, Mable?"

Yip! Yip!

"Where is Iggy? She sounds distressed."

"I know," Mable groaned, "She's locked in the spare bedroom."

"How did that happen?"

"I was working on my project, and I'd just finished the first couple of paragraphs. I needed to go to the bathroom. Iggy was in the room with me, and I had just given her a treat. I walked out of the bedroom, and I guess I was distracted because I shut the door behind me."

"The door locked?" Ethan asked.

"I must have bumped the lock at some point earlier."

"How long has it been?"

Mable checked her watch. "Um, like, three hours?"

Ethan put his palm on his forehead and shook his head. "Wow, I wish you had called me sooner."

Mable felt her cheeks burn. "I'm sorry. I tried to get the door open, but I couldn't find any key for it. I looked everywhere!" Her chest was tight now, and she put a hand to her chest and rubbed it.

Ethan frowned, "You don't have asthma, do you?"

"No," she said gasping.

Ethan stepped closer to her, and he put his hands on her shoulders. She liked the weight of his palms on her. His brown eyes looked into hers. "Mable, take a deep breath."

"I-I c-can't."

"Everything is going to be fine, but we don't want you to pass out. Try again, I'll count. Inhale one, two, three, four. And exhale one, two, three, four."

Mable looked at Ethan's face. She could see stubble dotting his firm jaw, and a few freckles on the bridge of his nose. She liked the way his nose sloped; she wanted to run her finger down it and then lean in and give him a kiss. But for now, she needed to breathe. They stood facing each other as Ethan counted, and Mable inhaled and exhaled for another minute.

Then little Iggy started howling.

"I didn't even know she could do that," Mable said.

Ethan shrugged and started walking down the hall to where Iggy was locked in. He stood at the door and began speaking softly. He put his hand on the door, and seconds later, Iggy had stopped howling.

Mable's heart swelled. He was so good at this. Ethan squatted down and looked at the doorknob.

She moved back to give him room. Mable found herself staring at the back of him. His dark hair was in short waves that skimmed down just about to the nape of his neck. She subconsciously leaned forward, licking her lips. He turned toward her quickly, and she jerked back.

"I think we can drill out the lock and get the door open. I'm going to look in the garage for a drill. You go look online for a video on how to do it. See if you can find a video showing as close to this exact door handle as possible."

"Got it!" Mable saluted Ethan and then felt like an idiot. What was wrong with her?

Ethan cocked his head. "Also, get some cheese and put a piece under the door for Iggy to eat. Find something to push it as far into the room as possible. If we're going to drill out the door handle, I want Iggy to be as far away from the door as we can manage."

Mable nodded. "I'll go see what I can find." Ethan turned to go to the garage, and Mable went into the kitchen. She took cheese out of the fridge, cut a couple of small pieces, and put them on a small plate. She went to the small pantry, looking for something she could use to push them far under the door. Mable scanned the shelves and found nothing. Her shoulders slumped. She took out the hair tie that was holding her braid, put it on her wrist, and undid her braid. Once her hair was undone, she ran her hands through it. "Think," she said out loud, "there must be something I can use." She looked around one more time and then she saw a couple of long marshmallow skewers hanging on the wall next to the light switch. Eyeballing the skewer, she figured it was almost a yard long.

Mable grinned and took one skewer off the wall. She went back into the kitchen and started looking for a how-to video to drill the lock on a door handle. It took a couple of different keyword searches, but shortly Mable found a three-minute video that showed a door handle with the same locking mechanism as the bedroom door.

Ethan walked into the kitchen with the cordless drill. Mable couldn't help but give him a long look, noticing how his biceps bulged. She'd never had a handyman fantasy before now. She felt her core heat.

"Did you find a video?"

"Yep, come see!"

He set down the drill and stood next to her. He was a millimeter from her as she pressed play. She turned her head to the side, and they were almost cheek to cheek. "Can you see?" she said, feeling desperate for him to be even closer to her. "Here, lean in." She turned slightly closer to him, and now they were touching from thigh to chest. He put a hand on her lower back. The warmth of his touch was like a brand on her back. She pressed skip to get past an ad, and the video started playing. She hoped he was paying attention to what the guy was doing, because all she could think about was turning into him, wrapping her arms around his waist, and leaning down to kiss his full lips.

As the video continued, her breathing synced with his. Ethan's hand on her back moved in little circles, and she wanted to melt into his touch. Iggy was whining in the bedroom, and that brought her back to the worries of the day.

"Man, we've got to get the poor pupper out of that room!" Mable said.

Ethan moved his arm around Mable's waist and gave her a small squeeze. "We've got this!" He picked up the drill and started walking down the hall. Mable picked up the long skewer and the cheese and followed him.

"I feel terrible that she's in there all alone, and now you're going to make scary noises." Mable put the pieces of cheese on the end of the skewer and pushed it under the door as far as she could.

"She's not barking," Mable whispered. Ethan quickly lined up the drill bit to one side of the circular plate that connected to the handle. As he drilled, metal and wood shavings fell on the floor. She cursed herself for not thinking of having the vacuum cleaner ready to suck up the mess so Iggy didn't get any shavings in her little paws. Mable rubbed her neck. So far, the dog-sitting had been a total failure. She didn't even want to think about what would have happened if she didn't have Ethan to bail her out. Ethan pulled out the drill and reinserted it on the other side of the handle. Once he started drilling again, Iggy began yipping. "We are almost done, Iggy!" Mable tried to reassure the dog.

Ethan pulled the drill out and set it to the side. "Now we should be able to get the door to unlock."

Mable got on her knees and pressed play on her phone. Ethan followed the video and in less than a minute, the door was opening.

"Thank goodness!" Mable said, and she jumped up and gave Ethan a big hug. She was tempted to linger in his embrace, but then a video started loudly autoplaying.

"Check out this one easy trick to open any inside door! Just use a BBQ skewer!"

"Wait, what?" Ethan said.

Mable picked up her phone and they both stared at the screen as Iggy ran around their feet.

"I could have gotten Iggy out hours ago?" Mable said.

"We didn't need to wreck their door?" Ethan said.

They both shook their heads.

"Now we know," Mable said.

Ethan gave her a side hug and then bent down and picked up Iggy.

"I'll vacuum the shavings. Can you take her outside?" Mable said.

"You got it!" Ethan said and ran the puppy outside.

Mable pushed the door to the guest bedroom fully open. She wasn't surprised to see that Iggy had had an accident in the room. Mable cleaned up the mess and vacuumed. Then she walked outside to where Ethan was teaching Iggy to play fetch.

"Once again, you've saved the day."

"It could have happened to anyone. Don't beat yourself up."

Mable crossed her arms and stared at Ethan. "Seriously, I'm terrible at this."

"Puppies are not as easy as everyone thinks. You're doing okay. Look how happy Iggy is."

A clap of thunder sounded, and Iggy ran under the deck.

"Well, shit," said Ethan.

Chapter Ten

♥

Ethan shivered; a wind had picked up from the west, rustling the leaves.

Mable's phone chimed with an alert. She looked at her phone and groaned.

"What's up?" Ethan said as he kneeled and started making smoochy noises, trying to lure Iggy out from under the deck before it thundered some more.

"Severe thunderstorm warning in effect for the next eight hours. High chances of strong winds, potential hail, and tornados," Mable read.

"I thought tornadoes were a spring thing."

"These days they can happen practically year-round."

Ethan looked up at the sky. "I just remembered. I rode my bike here."

"If you want, I can give you a ride home?"

Ethan shrugged. He had a rope toy, and he held it out toward Iggy, who was almost out from under the deck, "Let's play, Iggy." He shook the rope.

"But then we need to take Iggy in the car. I can't leave her alone here, especially if it's going to storm." Mable said.

"Would you feel better if I spent the night again?" Ethan said.

"You would do that?"

Ethan looked up at Mable; his eyes were soft, and he had a hint of a smile. Ethan couldn't help himself; he was giving Mable puppy-dog eyes.

"You are looking at me like Iggy does when she wants one of her training treats."

"Erm." He dropped his eyes. "Whatever works best for you."

Ethan cautiously pulled on the rope, and Iggy popped out from under the deck. She trotted up the stairs and started pawing at Mable's leg.

"Aww, do you want me to pick you up?"

Mable leaned down to pick up the energetic puppy, her long blond hair falling like a curtain covering her and Iggy. She stood up with Iggy in her arms.

Ethan looked on, and his heart sped up. She was gorgeous.

"Eww!" Mable said. "She just peed on me!"

Mable held the dog out away from her, handing Iggy to Ethan. He had a sudden flash of déjà vu, or really more of a wish for the future, imagining a world where Mable would hand off their newborn to him after a surprise bath time pee.

"Ugh!" Mable yelled and rushed into the bathroom.

Ethan stood outside the bathroom door, petting Iggy, who was panting hard. A clap of thunder sounded, and Iggy yipped.

The shower turned on, and Ethan listened to the sound of water running for a moment. He daydreamed about helping Mable take off her tank top. First, he'd tug on the waistband of her shorts, pulling him to her, and then he'd slide his hands up under the thin ribbed material of her tank. His hand would gently brush the side of her breast.

Crack!

Bark!

Iggy jumped out of his arms and landed on the carpet. She scrambled away into the main bedroom. His dream interrupted; he followed Iggy, who promptly jumped on the bed and started barking and clawing at Nicole's comforter. Ethan plopped down on the bed and started trying to calm the dog.

A few minutes later, Mable came into the bedroom. She was combing through her long blond hair. She had on an oversized T-shirt. He licked his lips. The hard points of her nipples were visible through the thin cotton. His pants grew tighter. Ethan rolled over onto his stomach so she wouldn't notice his attraction. She gathered the hem of her shirt and tied it. This only revealed more of her long legs. He wanted to run his hand up her tanned leg, then kiss a trail up from her knee, his tongue finding its way along the sensitive skin of her inner thigh and ultimately...

"Ethan," Mable said.

"What?" He answered.

"Did you hear me?"

"I'm sorry I was distracted. What did you say?"

"I said, so you're cool with spending the night?"

"Yes," he said.

"Because of the storms."

"Totally. These storms are intense."

Mable moved to sit on the edge of the bed. She smelled like a different flower today, a spring flower. *Lilacs? No, not that; it was another purple or pink flower. It was irises. Yes, that was it.* He breathed in her scent, and relief flooded his veins. She smelled so good, nothing like Becca. Becca had smelled like brown sugar and caramel. She'd had that scent in lotion, body wash, and even a perfume mist. It had been hell getting through the holiday season after they broke up. You didn't realize how pervasive those smells were in cookies and cakes until brown sugar and caramel made you nauseous.

"Ethan?"

"What's up?" He sat up and looked at her.

Mable was twisting her hands together. "Since Iggy seems to be okay for the moment." They both looked down at Iggy who was lying on her side trying to catch her own tail.

"Would it be terrible if I did some schoolwork? It's due in like ten days, and if I don't get it done, I'm screwed."

Ethan noticed she was clenching her jaw as she waited for him to respond. "Of course! I understand. I'll watch Iggy and you go write."

Mable relaxed and smiled. "Thank you so much. Before Iggy got locked in the guest room, I'd finally got my opening paragraph down the way I want it."

Ethan leaned back on the mound of pillows in front of the headboard. Iggy had stopped trying to catch her tail, and she hopped into Ethan's lap.

Mable shook her head. "She is such a silly dog."

Ethan petted Iggy. "Yes, she is," he said in a singsong voice. Then he looked at Mable, who was standing near the door. "Go on, she's fine, go write that paper!"

Mable blew him a kiss. "Thank you so much!"

Ethan just gave her a broad smile. *As if being with you could be a chore.*

Chapter Eleven

♥

Mable leaned back and rubbed her neck. The clock on her laptop read eleven twenty-three. She hadn't moved from her spot in three hours. She saved her document, even though she had autosave on, and stood up to go to the bathroom. Mable passed by the main bedroom and peeked in.

Ethan was sprawled across the comforter, fast asleep, and in the crook of his arm, Iggy was out cold. She sighed. Mable couldn't even put into words how grateful she was that Ethan had come to her rescue again. Not that she typically needed any rescuing, it was just that taking care of a puppy seemed to involve a set of skills she did not possess. She partially closed the door and went into the kitchen to refill her water bottle.

In the kitchen, she realized the wind was picking up again. Tree branches from the tree next to the front door were tapping on the picture window. She went to the front door and opened it to see what the incoming storm looked like. But since it was almost midnight, she couldn't see much of anything; however, she could smell ozone in the air. Her hair began floating, and she turned to run back into the house just as the tornado siren wailed.

She rushed into the house and to the bedroom where Iggy was now howling and Ethan was nowhere to be found. Her heart leaped into her throat. "Ethan!" She shouted and turned back into the hallway.

"Mable!" Ethan ran out of the spare room, holding her laptop. "I went to find you and I saw your laptop wasn't plugged into a surge protector."

Iggy was on the floor between them, howling. Mable reached down and picked her up. "Oh my gosh, she is shaking."

The siren wails continued. "We need to go to the bathroom. It's the only room without windows," Ethan said.

"Right," Mable said. She grabbed the phone charger out of the wall, and the three of them, along with her laptop, went into the bathroom to huddle. Ethan shut the door to the bathroom and slid down to the ground. Mable squished in next to him and that took up almost all the floor space.

Ethan looked at his phone's battery. "Crap, I fell asleep and forgot to put it on the charger. I've only got twenty percent."

"Here, give me your phone. I'll plug it in. I'm at like sixty percent, so we should be good. I'll put on the Channel Twelve live stream so we can hear when they give the all-clear."

Ethan handed Mable his phone. As he did, their hands touched, and static electricity zapped them both.

"My hair was flying around outside. There must be a lot of electricity in the air." Mable put the charger into his phone and then turned on the live stream.

Iggy was barking and panting.

"I don't think she likes storms," Mable said.

"If I had realized it was going to storm, I would have stopped at Petwise and gotten her a thundershirt."

"A thundershirt? Oh, wait, I've heard of that. It's to hug her so she won't be distressed. They have those for kids too."

Ethan smiled and nodded. "Exactly, just like that. See you are getting the hang of this."

Mable felt her cheeks flush. Ethan was so good at making her feel things. She had an idea to help Iggy calm down. She leaned over Ethan, and as she did, her breast brushed against his forearm. Her nipples hardened at this barest of touches, and she felt warms spread low in her belly. She squirmed a little, and that only made her more eager for contact with him. She reached up and pulled a hand towel off the counter. He touched her side, steadying her, and she briefly considered straddling his lap.

She lowered herself back down and sat next to him. Their legs were touching. He could move away from her, but he didn't. "Iggy," she said and made a kissing noise. Iggy hopped into her lap and whined. She was still shaking. Mable took the hand towel and wrapped Iggy up as if she were a baby.

Ethan looked down and shrugged. "It can't hurt."

In the background, the live stream of Channel Twelve continued. "We have a long line of thunderstorms entering the area from Iowa. These powerful storms have already produced several tornadoes, and the entire Chicagoland area is under a Tornado Warning until eight a.m. If you hear sirens, please go to a basement or an interior room and stay there. Illinois Power is reporting over a hundred thousand houses without power. It's likely that number will grow as the night goes on."

As if on cue, the light in the bathroom flickered and went off for a moment, then came back on. Ethan put his hand on Mable's thigh. She wondered if her hair was floating around her head again; she could feel electricity snapping between them. She placed her head on his shoulder. "Is this okay?"

"More than okay." His voice was hoarse. She breathed in his summer scent. Iggy grew restless in her arms, so she put the puppy down. Iggy went over to the bathmat next to the bathtub, did a few circles on the mat, and then laid down.

Ethan turned his head toward Mable, and he kissed the crown of her head. Her chest felt heavy with want, and she lifted her head. They were facing each other now. His breath was on her lips. She looked down at his full lips and the raspy stubble covering his chin. He lifted his hand and cupped her cheek. She closed her eyes and leaned into his hand. He traced her lips with his thumb.

"Mable," he said.

"Yes?" she said.

"Can I kiss you?"

"Please do."

He pressed his soft lips against hers, and it felt so good. She'd never been kissed so sweetly. He moved slightly, taking her bottom lip between his teeth, and it was like a direct line from his mouth to her pussy. A small moan escaped her lips and then his tongue entered her mouth. She met his tongue with hers, wanting to taste all of him. He pulled her toward him, and she leaned into his touch. She felt dizzy as the kiss continued. She turned her head and felt the scrape of his stubble against her chin.

"Mable," he murmured.

She wondered what it would be like if they went further. Would he shout her name as he came? He kissed her again, harder this time, and she matched him in intensity. Their tongues entwined, and she rubbed her legs together, trying to soothe the ache that was building within her. They came apart, panting. She put her forehead to his. His brown eyes were wild.

The lights flickered again and then went out. Thunder sounded and this time it felt like the entire house was shaking. Over the howling wind, the tornado sirens sounded again. Iggy howled and scurried up between them. She clawed at Ethan's shirt, pushing Mable away from him.

ETHAN

If Ethan weren't such a kindhearted lover of dogs and tamer of wayward puppies, he might have been inclined to call Iggy a real cockblocker. But that wasn't him. Besides, he had no clue what Mable was interested in. Perhaps it was just the emotions of the day that had electrified their kiss. He moved away from her and began soothing the dog.

Mable straightened her shirt and checked the Channel Twelve live stream. "I hope we don't have to wait too long for the electricity to come back on. My phone is down to forty percent."

Thunder began rolling again, and Iggy shivered and tried to paw her way into Ethan's chest. The room was dark aside from the light of Mable's phone. In the dim light, he watched her face; she squinted, and he loved how her nose scrunched up as she tried to read the screen. He was tempted to bop her on the nose and then kiss it. After that he'd move down and take her bottom lip and suck on it as his hands moved lower, cupping her small breasts. Just when he thought it couldn't possibly get hotter in the bathroom, here he was, sweat pouring down his back.

"Mable, what's the radar look like? Do you think the storms will be over soon? It's stifling in here."

Mable held the phone closer to her face, then she held it away and used her fingers to zoom in. "I think it's going to be over soon. The tornado warning is supposed—"

Mmmwahhhhhhh

"Great, there it goes again," Ethan said, dejected, and tried to console the howling Iggy.

A few minutes passed; they made soothing noises to calm Iggy. The heat and stress of the long day was getting to Ethan, and he closed his eyes for a moment. As he was drifting into sleep, he felt the delicious weight of Mable's head against his shoulder. Her hair draped onto his chest and as he slumbered, he dreamed he was being wrapped in a silken cocoon by a spider with warm brown eyes and a pert little nose.

Chapter Twelve

♥

Mable woke up and found herself with her head in Ethan's lap, which wasn't great, and what was worse than that was the wet spot she'd drooled on his crotch. She pushed up and looked at her phone. It was seven in the morning, and the weather warnings had expired. She plugged her phone into the charger, and it started charging.

She didn't want to wake Ethan, but she really, really needed to pee. Mable poked him in the shoulder, and he mumbled something she couldn't make out. She shook him now; her need to be polite overridden by her full bladder. "Ethan," she hissed.

His eyes opened, and he slowly focused on her. "Hey there," he said, smiling lazily, "What time is it?"

She tugged on his arm, trying to get him to stand up. "Time for you to leave this bathroom so I can pee."

"Sorry." His eyes grew big, and he scrambled up and out the door. Iggy followed him out.

"Can you let Iggy out? I'm sure she must have to go too!" she shouted through the door as she rushed over to the toilet.

"Will do!" Ethan said. "Cmon, Iggy girl! Let's get you outside."

Mable groaned in relief. Then she flushed the toilet, washed her hands, and took a couple of minutes to brush her teeth before exiting the bathroom to make some coffee.

She twisted her hair into a topknot and bustled around the kitchen, pulling the coffee beans out of the freezer, plugging in the grinder, and then setting the French press on the counter. She'd taken the time to watch a couple of videos on how to make French press coffee yesterday, and she'd learned it was surprisingly easy to make. At about the same time that she was adding the hot water to the press, the back door closed. The clickity-clack of Iggy's paws announced her arrival in the kitchen. She stood on the spot where Mable usually put her food bowl and gave a sharp bark.

"One moment, Miss Iggy, breakfast is coming up." Mable turned to get Iggy's food and walked right into Ethan. He reached out and put his hands on her waist before she slammed into him. She found herself almost annoyed at being denied full-body contact.

"Sorry about that," Ethan said. "I was going to get a glass of water." His hand lingered at her waist.

She couldn't help herself, and she leaned over and kissed him. He kissed her back, and before things could go further, Iggy yipped.

"Okay, okay, Iggy, we get it." She pulled away from Ethan and poured Iggy's food into her bowl and placed it where Iggy stood waiting impatiently.

"I have to tell you, even though I work at Jesse's Pub when I'm not at school, I don't really cook, like, at all." Mable said.

"No worries," Ethan said as he poured himself a cup of coffee. Then he opened the refrigerator and took out a stick of butter.

Mable watched in horror as Ethan added a tablespoon of butter to his fresh coffee. "Gross."

Ethan raised an eyebrow. "It's how I start my day."

Mable shook her head dramatically. "Next you'll tell me you are into intermittent fasting."

"Now that you mention it."

"Oh no," she said, putting her hand against her forehead in mock distress.

"It's true," he whispered. "I usually only eat between eight and four."

"I don't know about you," Mable said with a smile.

Ethan looked at the clock on the stove. "It's five after eight. Is there anything in the fridge I can whip up for us to have for breakfast, or do we need to go over to Donnie's?"

"Um," Mable said, biting her lip.

Ethan took a sip of his coffee. "Well then, what if we take Iggy on a little walk over to Donnie's and enjoy a bagel or muffin for breakfast?"

"So you do eat carbs?"

"If it means I get to have breakfast with you, I do."

Mable felt heat rise up her neck. "Let's go then, but first I need to change. I hope you don't mind."

"Not at all!" Ethan said.

Mable stood in the bedroom, trying to decide what to wear. When she'd packed to stay at Sean and Nicole's, she'd been in a hurry and she'd just thrown a bunch of tank tops, T-shirts, and shorts in her bag. She should have brought a couple of sundresses. Then again, she was just going to grab some breakfast with Ethan. This wasn't a date. This was only a couple of newly friendly people enjoying a meal together because they happened to be hungry at the same time.

Even though she knew nothing was going to happen, she rummaged through her bag until she found a matching set of underwear, a baby blue strapless bra and bikini-cut panties. She topped that with a light purple scoop-neck T-shirt and her favorite cut-offs. She quickly plaited her hair in a side braid and threw on mascara.

When she went back out to the kitchen, Ethan was putting their coffee cups in the dishwasher. He looked up at her and paused for a moment. "You look beautiful."

She felt her cheeks warm. Mable bit her bottom lip to stop herself from dismissing his compliment. She looked at him but avoided his eyes; instead, she focused on his mouth. He lazily smiled, and butterflies fluttered in her stomach. She loved the little brackets around his smile. She longed to trace them with her fingers.

"Thanks," she said simply, afraid her tongue would get tied if she tried to say anything more. "Are you ready to go?"

Ethan made a show of looking down at himself and then smelling under his armpits. He moved toward her. "I think I'm good. Wanna check?"

Mable leaned in a little and took a hesitant sniff. She could still smell a hint of chlorine and coconut. "You smell like you."

Ethan glanced at her sideways. "Is that a good thing?"

"Yep," she said, and she walked away to get Iggy's leash, hiding the big smile on her face.

Chapter Thirteen

♥

As they walked toward Donnie's shop. Iggy wanted to stop and smell all the flowers, rocks, grass, and debris they came across. Before they'd made it a block, Iggy had managed to wrap the leash around her legs, as well as Mable's legs. Ethan bent down and helped untangle Iggy from Mable. As she held still, he brushed his hand down her leg, feeling her soft skin and wishing they could turn around and spend the morning discovering each other.

He felt warmth low in his belly. At the same time, he didn't know if he should embrace what he was feeling for Mable. His breathing turned shallow; he could not handle another Becca situation. He wasn't built to withstand it. Once the leash was untangled, they resumed walking, but it didn't take long for Iggy to tangle herself again.

"Can I show you how to hold the leash so she learns how to walk with us?" He said.

"That would be great. What I'm doing now is really not working."

They paused at the corner of Main Street. It was a quiet morning, and hardly anyone was out and about.

His throat tightened. Being near her flustered him. "You want to shorten the leash here." He moved Mable's thumb to the button. She depressed it. "We want Mable to learn to stay by our side and not run ahead of us. We are the leaders and we need to show her we're in charge."

"I think she knows who is in charge."

"Yeah, and it's not us," Ethan chuckled and ran a hand through his hair, "So let's change that now."

"Right." Mable nodded.

Ethan moved into her space again. He couldn't help but breathe her in. He wondered how she would taste, and he needed to cut off that line of thinking right away. The flimsy shorts he was wearing could not hide an erection. "Hold it like this in two hands. He moved her other hand. If she gets ahead of us, we are going to stop. Then we will make eye contact with her and say no."

"Do you think this is going to work?"

"It should, but then again, Iggy is something else."

"She's got an enormous personality in that tiny body," Mable said.

"Yes, she does. Ready?"

Mable steeled herself dramatically, and they began to walk up Main Street.

"Really, Iggy?" Mable said as they watched Iggy sniff around the door of New Age Stones and Witch Crafts.

"Has she been here before?"

"I brought her here. My friend Hannah was working. I guess she's checking to see if she can smell herself?"

Ethan nodded. "Hannah? Is she the redhead?"

"Yes, you know her?"

"No, not really. I think we met once at Hop's Heaven. She seems nice."

"She's the best. C'mon, Iggy," Mable tugged lightly and Iggy moved away from the storefront.

They walked the rest of the way to Donnie's Books and Breads and only had to stop twice when people paused to fawn over Iggy. She was the kind of dog that even cat lovers asked if they could pet.

Mable blushed, "I know, she is super cute, and I would love to let you pet her, but she likes to nip at, like, everyone, and I don't want her to sink her teeth into you!"

The jogger who'd stopped in her tracks and bent down to pet Iggy halted mid-bend and stood up. "That seems pretty hard to believe." She crossed her arms.

Ethan put on his best smile. "She's chomped a few of my fingers."

The woman pouted. "I guess I better keep my hands to myself."

"Yep," Mable said, and then she bit her lip.

Ethan shook his head. The jogger huffed and started running again.

"I'm sorry, I shouldn't have said anything, but I couldn't help myself. She was acting like she knew Iggy better than me!"

"She was being a jerk. Maybe we should have let her pet Iggy."

Mable burst out laughing. "Iggy would have totally bitten her!"

"Yep," Ethan said, mimicking the tone Mable used on the jogger. "Here we are."

"Are you sure it's okay to have dogs in the bakery?" Mable's eyebrows were knit together.

"Good question. I didn't even think of that. Do you want to sit outside, and I'll go in and order, and we'll eat on the patio?"

Mable looked relieved. She sat down and Iggy went under her chair. "Oh, no! She's probably so thirsty! Can you get her some water? And something for her to drink it out of?"

"Yep, got it. Now what do you want to eat?"

"Just get me whatever you're getting."

"Okay, a red-eye coffee with some butter and a side of bacon."

"No, not that!" She scrunched up her nose and frowned.

Ethan laughed. "You still look cute, even when you're disgusted."

Mable smiled shyly, and then her stomach growled.

Ethan stood straighter. "I'll go get our food—how about two lavender cold brews and everything bagels with cream cheese?"

"That would be amazing." She put her hand in her back pocket and pulled out her debit card. "Here is my card."

Ethan waved her off, "I got it." He turned around to go into the bakery. In the reflection of the bakery door, he could see Mable was watching him, and her eyes were firmly on his ass. He grinned and walked into the bakery.

Only one table remained open, so it was just as well that they were eating outside. Donnie was filling a box of donuts for a customer. When he saw Ethan, he waved a gloved hand at him.

Ethan waved back. "Hi, Donnie!"

The door chimed and a moment later, someone clapped Ethan on the shoulder. "Hey bro," Jax said.

"Jax, what are you up to?" Ethan said.

Jax tossed their black hair with red tips over their shoulder. "I went to the beauty school and got my hair refreshed."

"Looks great, the red is new, isn't it?"

"Yeah, I thought I'd try something new, only a couple of months until the spooky season."

"Planning to be a vampire for Halloween?"

"Maybe."

"It's too soon to be talking about the fall. I'm trying to enjoy my summer vacation here."

"How's it going with the boys on vacation? Are you sleeping in? Going clubbing? We should get together and play cards."

"Actually, I've been helping Mable watch Sean and Nicole's puppy."

"They got a puppy? I thought they were in Scotland."

"Day before they were leaving for their honeymoon, they adopted a stray. She's outside on the patio with Mable."

Jax squinted and looked closer at Ethan.

Ethan avoided their gaze and looked over at the bakery counter.

"So, you're spending your vacation helping Mable with a puppy." Jax paused and put a finger to their chin.

Ethan shrugged. "Looks like it is my turn to order." He gave his order to the employee working with Donnie and then waited for Jax to order before continuing.

"She is clueless about how to take care of Iggy. I had to help her."

"Had to?" Jax said. They both moved over to the pickup end of the counter and waited for their orders. "I'm sorry, I'm just messing with you, Ethan. If I'm being honest, I've got to tell you, this is the happiest I've seen you since we met."

"Thanks. I feel like I'm in a really good place right now."

"And how much of that has to do with Mable?"

"We are having fun, but I don't think either of us is up for anything more than being friends."

"Jax, your order is up!" Donnie said.

Jax took his iced coffee and bakery bag out of Donnie's hand. "Thanks, Donnie, have a good one."

"You too, Jax! See you at book club next month!"

"Can't wait!" Jax said. Then Jax turned back to Ethan. "You know, it's okay to date someone casually. It doesn't have to be that serious."

"Says the person who's been with their partner for what? Five years now?"

Jax smiled widely. "Yep, it was five years last month. But that doesn't mean I'm wrong. If you like Mable, why not ask her out?"

Ethan nodded. "Maybe I will."

"Keep me posted and let me know when you want to get together and play cards."

"I'm free every night until the twins come home."

"Let's plan for a Monday night?"

"Perfect, I'll text you," Ethan said.

Jax walked out of the bakery. Ethan rocked back on his feet, considering what Jax had said. Could he manage to just have some fun? Did Mable want a casual relationship? He frowned. He was bad at casual. The only thing he knew how to do was how to fall hard and get hurt. How could he manage to keep things fun and light? It was probably better to avoid it altogether and not go any further with Mable.

"Ethan! Ethan! Your order is up!" Donnie said.

Ethan took his order from the counter. "Sorry about that. I was daydreaming."

"About a certain beautiful blonde?"

Ethan shook his head and picked up the drinks and bagels. He walked to the door and went outside. Mable waved. *Her smile wrecks me.* His chest ached as he closed the space between them and set down their breakfast.

"Shoot, I forgot to get a bowl and water for Iggy." He pushed his chair back and stood up.

"No, you sit. I'll go get it." Mable smiled and got up.

He took a sip of his iced coffee. Mable was back a few seconds later.

"Donnie says he'll bring out some water for Iggy." Mable sat down at the table and took a long drink of her iced coffee. "This is so good. I love lavender in iced coffee."

He smiled and scooted his chair closer to Mable's. Even though he'd tried to talk himself into just being friends with Mable, he could not stay in the friend zone. He was about to put his hand on Mable's knee when the bakery door jingled, and Donnie came out. Ethan leaned back in his chair, away from Mable.

"Where's the new puppy? I've got some nice fresh water for her." Donnie bent down, his knees cracking, and he poured water into a small dog bowl. "Mind if I join you two for a few minutes?"

"No, please join us!" Mable said. "Would you like some of my bagel? Are you hungry?"

Donnie patted his belly. "I would, but I'm trying to work on limiting my carbs."

Mable cocked her head. "I don't know how I feel about a baker who is avoiding carbs."

Donnie chuckled, "I'm trying to eat them in moderation. I could never go without them. I turn into a bear when I don't get my grains and starches! Is Iggy hungry? I usually try to keep Scooby snacks in stock, but it's been busy on the book side. Can you believe Books and Breads is the first stop on Charlie Donlea's book tour next month?"

"I can't say I've heard of him, but I read little outside of picture books these days," Ethan said.

Mable shook her head. "All I read are textbooks."

"No worries, you both can come to the book signing. He's going to read an excerpt from his latest thriller, and I'm sure you'll be hooked."

Donnie rubbed his beard. "Gah! I'm so excited!"

"I'm sure it's going to be a colossal hit," Mable said.

Donnie smiled at Mable, fine lines crinkling around his light brown eyes.

Yip, yip! Iggy stood on her hind legs and pawed Donnie's meaty calves. He picked up the little puppy and put her in his lap. She promptly sat down and nudged his hand to be petted.

Mable and Ethan's mouths dropped. They were speechless.

Donnie looked up at the couple, "What?"

"She's been biting everyone who tries to pick her up or pet her, and she just let you do both," Ethan said. He leaned toward Donnie, "If this gets out, I'm going to lose my street cred as the dog and kid whisperer of Marley Creek."

Donnie gave a big, booming laugh. Iggy looked up at him and barked. He went back to petting her. "Dogs and me, we get along. Now cats, that's another story. Maybe if I sold tuna instead of cupcakes? When it comes to kids, there isn't enough time in the day to go into that."

"How's Bastian?"

"Same as it always is. He's fifteen and thinks I'm an idiot."

Mable patted Donnie's hand. "If it helps at all, that's a very normal stage of development."

Donnie sighed and rubbed his chin. "Thanks, Mable, I suppose it's good to know that it's a stage, and he's on track. Ever since Maggie died, I've tried to do everything I can to help Bastian with his emotional development."

Ethan crumpled up the paper his bagel had been sitting on. "You're an awesome dad, Donnie."

"Thanks, buddy, but enough about me. How's everything with you two?"

Ethan glanced at Mable, whose chest was flushed red. She took a bite of her bagel, so he answered Donnie's question. "Not that you would know it right now, but Iggy has been a real handful, and this is Mable's first time dog-sitting. She asked me for some help and since the twins are in Atlanta, I've been able to help with this demon dog."

"Demon dog? This sweet puppy who's fast asleep on my lap?"

"Yes, her. Do you see how she's acting? Like a perfect angel for you right now, but if you could see her at home —she's destroyed one of the throw pillows, and this morning I noticed one of the kitchen table chairs had teeth marks on it. She's gnawing the furniture!" Mable said.

"It's a good thing Iggy is so cute," Ethan said, looking at Mable.

"Exactly," she said.

Mable's eyes were lingering on Ethan, and he clenched his fists, fighting the urge to reach over and brush his knuckles over her cheek and tuck a loose strand of hair behind her ear.

"Are you staying at Sean and Nicole's until they come back, Ethan?"

"Um," Ethan started, unsure how to answer. "No, well, actually, it just depends on what Mable prefers."

Donnie continued petting Iggy. "What do you think, Mable?"

Mable frowned slightly, and then she turned to address Ethan instead of answering Donnie. "I hate to sound selfish, but you've been such a help, I'm finally getting some work done on the paper. Could you stay longer and help with Iggy?" Mable bit her bottom lip.

Ethan grinned like a fool. "Definitely." He nodded his head. "I'm happy I can help. I could even proofread if you want."

Mable laughed. "You're the best. I don't want to take advantage of you, since you're already helping so much."

Donnie looked back and forth between the two, who had forgotten his six-foot-two, extra-large self was still sitting at their table.

Ethan looked away from Mable, suddenly too shy to look directly into her eyes. "I enjoy being with you, and Iggy, of course."

Mable licked her lips. "I enjoy spending time with you too." She fidgeted with the straw in her cold brew.

"Then I guess I should stay?" Ethan asked hopefully.

Mable nodded. "I would like that. You probably need to go get some clothes and stuff. We can drive over this afternoon?"

Ethan smiled, his eyes lighting up. "That would be great." A cooling breeze blew through the patio, and a napkin went flying off their table. Ethan and Mable followed the napkin as it flew. Ethan jerked back slightly as he realized his friend, Donnie, was still at the table. He'd been so focused on Mable, everything else had become background. Mable got up and chased down the napkin, then she cleaned off the table where they were sitting.

"Well, I better get back to work. Time to bake the donuts, as they say," Donnie told them.

"Talk to you later," Ethan said.

"Good to see you, Mable," Donnie said.

"Thanks for the water," Mable said.

"Anytime. Have a splendid afternoon, you two." Donnie deposited Iggy in Ethan's lap and left the table.

"What should we do now? Mable asked.

<h1 style="text-align:center">Chapter Fourteen</h1>

♥

Mable rolled her head on her shoulders, trying to release some of the tension that had come from sitting and typing all afternoon. After they'd finished their breakfast, they'd walked back to the house, and then Mable had driven Ethan home so he could pack a bag. Ethan didn't have a car himself; he used the Belmont's minivan. They'd told him he could use it while they were gone, but he preferred not to take it over to sit in Sean and Nicole's driveway.

Once they'd returned, he'd offered to monitor Iggy for the afternoon so Mable could work on her project, and she'd managed to get three pages written as well as a solid outline for her video presentation. She inhaled and realized someone was cooking.

"Is Ethan cooking dinner?" She asked the room. Her heart swelled, and her mouth watered. She checked the time and saw that it was already past five. It had been ages since they'd had those bagels for breakfast. She walked down the hall to the kitchen and burst out laughing. Ethan had on an apron that said "Mr. Good Looking Is Cooking!" Since it was Sean's apron and

Sean was at least six inches taller and fifty pounds heavier, Ethan was swimming in the apron.

"What's cooking, Mr. Good Looking?"

Ethan did a little shimmy and went back to the stove. Mable moved into the kitchen and looked over his shoulder. "What are we having for dinner?"

"I found some ground turkey in the freezer and they had pasta and sauce in the cabinet, so I thought I haven't had spaghetti in ages. I hope you like spaghetti."

"I love it, especially if I don't have to make it."

"How about you set the table and see if they have any cheap wine?"

"Right, Sean will kill us if we drink the good stuff," Mable said.

"If he knew the hard time we've been having with Iggy, he might be okay with us having a nice glass of wine."

They looked at each other, and Mable nodded. "I'll look for the cheap stuff."

Mable opened the cabinet and began pulling out plates and silverware. Once she'd completed that task, she realized Iggy wasn't in the kitchen begging for food. "Where's Iggy?"

Ethan turned from the stove and pointed to the living room. "She's in the living room watching *Bluey*."

"No way."

Ethan nodded, "Way."

"Does this mean we've found her kryptonite?"

"Here's hoping!" A timer buzzed, and Ethan turned back to the stove.

Mable opened the wine and poured a couple of glasses. She took her glass and walked quietly toward Iggy. The dog was sprawled out in front of the children's show, sound asleep. Mable stifled the urge to do a happy dance, lest she spill her wine.

She walked back to the table and sat down. Propping her elbow on the table, she rested her chin on her hand. She watched Ethan drain the pasta, admiring his broad shoulders. He was so fit; she imagined running her hands over his shoulders and then touching his biceps. Her core heated as she wondered what it would be like to press herself against his solid chest. She licked her lips, thinking about the kisses they'd shared during the storm. Ethan put ladles in the bowls and brought them over to the table. Mable took another drink of her wine and watched him take off the apron and set it on the counter. Underneath, he was wearing a formfitting v-neck T-shirt and a pair of shorts that were just the way she liked, short enough to show off his thighs. Her mouth watered.

"Do you want me to fix you a plate?" Ethan asked.

Mable shook her head. "Ethan, you are the freaking best. I'm so glad you're here. No, you don't have to fix me a plate. I should make one for you!"

"Thanks, I appreciate you."

"Let's toast," she said.

"What are we toasting?"

"Rambunctious puppies falling asleep to *Bluey?*"

"I'll drink to that!" Ethan said, and they clinked glasses.

Mable filled her plate with pasta and then ladled on the sauce and ground turkey meatballs. Ethan did the same but went heavier on the meatballs and lighter on the pasta. Mable took a big bite of food; she was starving. "Everything tastes delicious," she said around a forkful of meatball.

"I'm glad you like it. I haven't cooked for anyone in ages."

"You're pretty good at it. I wouldn't have guessed based on when you worked at Jesse's Pub for those few weeks this past winter."

"It's much easier to make pasta from a box and sauce from a jar than to work in a restaurant, that's for sure."

"That's a good point."

They ate quietly. The only sound for a while was *Bluey* in the background. Then Mable spoke. "When Sean and Nicole asked me to watch Iggy, I was super excited not only because it meant I could work on my project some place quiet, but because it meant I would get to be alone and have my own space for two whole weeks."

Ethan put his fork down, and his mouth turned down.

Mable held up a finger. "The thing is, growing up I've always had to share a room with someone else. I commuted as an undergrad, and even this summer I was in a dorm-style building in Germany."

"Geez, I feel terrible. All you wanted was to be alone, and here I am practically moving in." Ethan pushed his chair back a little.

"Wait," she said and put her hand over his. "Let me finish. I'm so happy you are here! I don't know how I would have made it through the last few days without you! At a minimum, I would have rushed Iggy to the emergency vet and called Sean and Nicole in a panic during their honeymoon. Plus, I'd still be on page one of my paper. Instead, you came along, and I'm seeing a light at the end of this project tunnel. Like I can't thank you enough."

Ethan flipped his hand over, so they were holding hands now. "I don't know what to say."

Mable took a leap and blurted out her thoughts without a filter. "What if you kissed me instead of talking?"

Ethan looked stunned, but he quickly recovered and pulled her chair, so Mable was beside him. "Come here, you," he said, and then he put his finger under her chin and tilted Mable's head. He kissed her, his lips smashing against hers, and she matched his want with her own. She ran her hands through his hair, pulling him closer to her. He moaned into her mouth, and she pushed her tongue into his mouth, needing to taste more of him. As they kissed, he moved his hand from her waist and slid it up her side. She could not help herself and she turned into his touch, aching for his hand on her breast. He stroked his hand over her breast and then zeroed in on her pebbled nipple. He brushed the hardened nub with his thumb, and then she was moaning into his mouth.

"Oh, Ethan," she gasped as he moved his other hand. The sensation of the thin fabric of her shirt rubbing against her nipples was making her wet. She wanted to feel his tongue on her breasts. Ethan stopped to take a breath, then he moved down to kiss her neck. She felt need growing low in her belly. She leaned her head down and kissed the crown of his head. He was kissing her collarbone now. Each kiss left a trail of fire on her skin.

She ran her hand through his thick, russet hair. He moved lower and sucked on her nipple. His tongue swirling around the nub over the wet fabric. She was so wet she squirmed in her seat, certain he could smell her desire. Then he gave the same attention to her other breast. She rocked against him as he licked her. Ethan nipped her swollen nub through her shirt and she gasped in pleasure. She felt like she was on the brink of coming already, and they still had all their clothes on.

Mable put her hands on his thighs and tentatively slipped them under the hem of his shorts. The hair on his legs was coarse against her palms, and she liked the feeling. She wondered what it would be like to have all of him against her. Ethan moved up and was now kissing along the other side of her collarbone. He made his way up her neck, and then he sucked lightly on the sensitive skin below her earlobe. She shivered as he blew lightly on the spot he'd sucked. He must have felt her shiver because she heard a low chuckle rumble in his throat. That just turned her on more. She sighed against him, and he moved back to reclaim her mouth. The rasp of his beard scratched against her chin. Mable stopped the kiss for a moment and rubbed her cheek against his, enjoying the sandpaper roughness against her tender skin. She needed to know what it would be like to have those cheeks rubbing against her thighs and his tongue exploring her. But before any of that could happen, they needed to talk.

She turned back and kissed his soft lips, and this time, before things could get any more heated, she broke off the kiss and pulled back.

"We need to talk about this." She pointed between the two of them.

Ethan looked up at her through his bangs. "Of course."

Once again, she spoke without bothering to filter her thoughts. "I'm up for some fun, but not sex."

Chapter Fifteen

♥

When Mable had said she didn't want to have sex, she probably expected him to be disappointed. However, it almost made him glad. He wasn't sure he could handle having sex with anyone yet. "Fun but no sex, got it. I mean, whatever you feel comfortable with, that works for me. I'm one hundred percent okay with whatever you want to do. You just let me know."

Mable smiled and gave Ethan's leg a squeeze. Ethan felt her smile down to his toes. He didn't know how she did it, but she smiled with her eyes. It was the cutest thing he thought he'd ever seen. Tucking her hair behind her ear, he cupped her face with his hand. Ethan couldn't touch her enough. He wanted to touch and kiss every inch of her body. More than anything Ethan wanted to be between her legs, kissing the very core of her and making her scream his name.

Mable took a deep breath, and he thought she seemed a little nervous to say what she needed.

"Seriously, whatever you need, I'm all for it," he repeated.

"When I say no sex, I mean like we can fool around and I'm definitely down for oral, but I don't want to have sex with you. The baby-making kind."

Ethan pursed his lips. "Not a problem! If that's what you prefer, I'm totally cool with that."

Mable sighed in relief. "I was afraid you'd be disappointed."

"Are you kidding? No way."

"Well, then." She put her hand on his chest and moved it slowly down to his waist.

He took her hand in his and stood up. She followed him, and he led her down the hallway to the guest bedroom. Once they were in the room, he let her lead him to the bed. She sat down and he sat next to her. She began kissing him gently. As they kissed he said, "I could honestly do this all day." He placed his forehead against hers and dared to look into her eyes. Her eyes were filled with desire, and he hoped she could see the want for her in his. "God, you're beautiful," he said.

Her cheeks flushed. She moved back from him and pulled off her tank top. She was bare to him from the waist up. His mouth went dry as he feasted with his eyes. She had small, teardrop-shaped breasts. Her creamy skin was begging him to taste it . Her areolas were the same shade as strawberry ice cream. Strawberry ice cream was his favorite. He hoped Mable would become his new favorite flavor. He bent down and kissed his way to where the cream-colored skin moved into strawberry. Ethan swirled his tongue around the delicate pink flesh, and Mable gasped when he took her pebbled nipple into his mouth and sucked gently, and then harder as she fisted his hair.

"Mmm, that feels so good," Mable said hoarsely. She took her hand and began touching her other breast. The taste of her in his mouth, knowing she was touching herself was making him so hard he ached. He used one hand to adjust himself. He moved back, and Mable stopped.

"No, Mable, keep going," he said.

She pushed backward and moved up so that she was now sitting on the bed, with pillows and a headboard behind her. She rolled the nipple that was slick from his ministrations between her fingers, and he could not help but touch himself through his shorts. "You are so hot right now; do you know that?"

She laughed. "No, I don't think I do."

"My mouth is watering. I can't wait to taste your perfect pink pussy."

"How do you know it's perfect?"

"Look how gorgeous your breasts are, so pink and soft and just the right size. I know the rest of you is going to blow my mind."

Mable smiled a lazy smile. "Let's find out."

Ethan knelt on the bed beside Mable and put his hands on the waistband of her shorts. "Can I?" he asked.

"Yes, please."

He dragged off her shorts, leaving her clad only in a baby-blue thong. "Shit, you look good."

She blushed, "Take off your shirt."

"Yes, ma'am," he said.

He pulled off his shirt and tossed it across the room, where it landed next to a hamper. "You want me to take off my pants too? Make things even?"

"That only seems fair." Mable nodded.

He hopped off the bed and shucked off his shorts, leaving him wearing a pair of boxer briefs. Mable looked him up and down. "You look like a Greek statue."

He flexed his biceps for her, and she giggled. He kneeled on the bed and pushed her knees apart. Ethan maneuvered himself between her legs. He'd been dreaming about this moment. He started kissing behind her knee.

"That's nice. I like that," Mable said.

Warmth flooded Ethan's chest; he loved that she didn't hesitate to tell him what she liked this time. He moved up her leg with his mouth, slowly kissing and giving teasing licks. As he got closer to her core, her legs trembled, and he felt each shiver go through Mable and down into him. His cock was twitching now, but this wasn't about him. It was about her and her beautiful, wet pussy that he was so close to tasting.

He was at the crease where her inner thigh met her core now. He moved the barely there fabric of her thong with his finger and then traced her folds. Ethan slowly pressed closer to her clit, and she squirmed, trying to get more of him in her. "I want to hear you moan," he said.

"Ethan," she said breathily. And she reached down and moved his finger so it was on her clit, and then she guided his hand. Once he had her rhythm down, she moved her hand away.

He grabbed her hand and slowly sucked her juices off her hand. "You taste amazing, like honey."

Mable sat up and kissed him long and hard while he stroked her until she rocked against him. Her breathing was rapid now, and she was gripping his shoulders.

"Wait, baby, don't come yet." He moved away, and she whimpered. He went to the side of the bed. "Come here," he said, and she turned toward him. He pushed her legs apart and pulled her closer to him. She lifted her ass off the bed and he slid off her thong. She was finally bare in front of him.

"Baby, I was right. Your pussy is perfect."

Mable threw an arm across her face. "I'm so embarrassed."

Hard as it was to pause when she was laid out there in front of him. He stopped himself from diving in to lap up her juices.

"Embarrassed? But why? You're gorgeous."

"If I would have known where this was going, I would have shaved or gotten waxed."

"No need, baby, everything about you is just right."

"Are you sure?"

"Abso-fucking-lutely."

"Thanks, Ethan."

"Would you like me to continue now? Can I make you come with my name on your lips?"

"Yes, please."

He went back down, caressing her thighs before he finally slid his tongue through her folds, tasting the honey sweetness right from its source. She was rocking now, and he sucked on her swollen nub.

"Oh, yes, yes."

He continued to suck on her clit as he pressed one finger inside her. He felt her muscles tighten around his finger. She bore down, pressing into him, and he loved it.

"Oh my God, Ethan. Yes, that's the spot right there." She fisted her hands in his hair, pushing him further into her.

He took a second finger and slowly worked it into her pussy. She rocked against his hand. Her muscles were so tight around his fingers. He imagined what it would be like to have his cock in their place, and he almost came. His tongue stroked her clit while his fingers moved in and out of her, and then she was coming. Her pussy muscles clenched his fingers while she shouted.

"That's it, just like that! Yes! Ethan! Yes!" He slowed his movements, easing out of her and lazily laving her through her aftershocks. She slowly took her hands out of his hair. He leaned back, savoring another look at that perfect pink pussy of hers, and she sat up, putting her hands on his face, and kissed him. He shared the taste of her. Then she pulled back, and they sat forehead to forehead.

"That was—"

He finished "amazing?"

"I was going to say earth-shattering in the best way."

He kissed her, tugging gently on her lower lip in agreement.

She rolled back onto the bed, satiated. "Come here," she said, holding out her hand. She moved back, making room for him. He lay down facing her and pushed her hair out of her face.

Ethan cupped her face with his hand, and she rubbed against it. She threw her leg over his hip, pushing him so close to her he felt like he was about to come from the sudden friction on top of getting off on eating her out.

"Do you know what you are doing to me?" he asked as he tried to think about non-sexy things like the time he dropped a tray of beer glasses at Hop's Heaven.

"Mm-hmm," she said, and she positioned herself so that she was lined up with the hardened length of him. Less than an hour ago, he'd been glad she hadn't wanted to have sex. And now he found himself feral with desire. He'd love nothing more than to roll them over and then to sheath himself in her wet pussy, but he respected her boundaries and so he let her do what she wanted with him. She rubbed herself against him, and he knew he wasn't going to last.

He looked into her eyes, and they sparkled with joy. It pushed him to the brink to see her realize the power she had over him. "Baby," he gasped.

"Come for me," she whispered. That was all he needed to hear. He thrust against her warmth through the thin fabric of his underwear and within seconds, he was coming harder than he could remember. "Baby, so good," he shouted.

Mable ran her hand down his back, letting her nails lightly scratch him as he shuddered. "My God, Mable." He said, unable to say anything coherent.

She smiled at him and nodded. "I know. That was pretty amazing."

He grinned. They lay together for a little while, and then Iggy came running into the room. She scratched at the bed.

"I'll take care of her," Mable said. "You probably want to take a shower."

He kissed Mable and got off the bed.

Before heading to the shower, he picked up Mable's clothes off the floor and handed them to her.

She threw on her shirt and shorts. "Come on, Miss Iggy, time to go potty."

Ethan listened to the soft sound of Mable walking toward the back door in combination with the click of Iggy's nails on the ceramic tile. The door creaked open, and then they were outside. He walked to the main bedroom to get his clothes and use the ensuite shower. Before getting into the shower, he looked in the mirror. He had to admit he looked rested and happy. He'd forgotten about all the good that came from being with someone, dating someone.

Was he dating Mable? No, she'd said she wanted to have some fun. Then again, wasn't the phrase casual dating all about having some fun? Ethan hung his towel on the rack and reflected. He'd had such a shit time with Becca, and that was putting it mildly. He liked Mable, and all he needed to do this time was not to fall for her. She just wanted to have fun and not have sex. Ethan could deliver that. If they only made out for the rest of their time together with Iggy, he'd be happy.

He needed to remember, things didn't have to be so serious. Ethan stepped into the shower, and as he lathered up, he couldn't stop thinking about Mable, her lips on his, the pink of her nipples, the way it had turned him on when she moaned against him. Instantly, he was hard again. He lathered up his hands and began stroking himself, replaying the way Mable had come on his face. Even over the soap's fragrance, the honeyed scent of Mable filled his senses. He bit his bottom lip to stop from shouting as he came. As he toweled off, he realized he should have shouted his orgasm. Mable should know what she did to him.

Chapter Sixteen

♥

The stress and the fun of the last few days had caught up with her and Ethan. After she'd had her shower, they'd gone into the living room and started watching a movie. Within ten minutes of starting the film, Mable couldn't stop yawning, which made Ethan yawn.

"I was thinking, there's no sense for you to be sleeping all the way over there in the main bedroom, in that big, giant bed when I have such a nice, cozy bed across the hall."

Ethan tilted his head. "Will there be cuddling?"

"So much cuddling."

"Okay, I'm down for that." He picked up the remote and clicked off the TV. She stood up, practically weaving on her feet. Iggy stretched and hopped off her doggy bed. She wagged her tail and waited for Ethan and Mable to walk to the bedroom. She rushed ahead of them and when they walked into the room, Mable was surprised to see her in the middle of the bed.

"I didn't think she could get on the bed. She always pawed at the comforter, waiting to be lifted onto the bed."

"She was doing the same thing in the other bedroom, but that bed is still too tall for now. I guess she's learned something new."

"I hope Sean and Nicole won't mind her jumping on the bed."

"Didn't you say Nicole was going to buy Iggy an entire wardrobe in Scotland?"

"Yep," Mable said.

"I think it's clear who the boss of this house is, and it ain't a human."

Mable giggled. She pulled back the comforter and got into bed. She laid down on her side. Ethan climbed into bed behind her and wrapped his arm around her. Mable liked the weight of him surrounding him. "I like having you as my big spoon."

"Me too, w-well, I mean I enjoy getting to be your big spoon."

Iggy moved to the end of the bed next to Ethan's feet and made three circles before lying down. Little doggy snores soon emanated from her.

Mable put her hand in Ethan's. His breath was on her neck and instead of being annoyed by it, she found it comforting.

Just as she was drifting off, Ethan spoke.

"Mable, are you still awake?"

"Mm-hmm," she said, and she turned so she was on her back. Ethan propped himself up on his elbow and looked down at her. "Can we talk?"

Mable's stomach clenched, "Sure," she said.

"Back in October, my girlfriend dumped me. We'd been together for a couple of years."

"Oh," Mable said, her stomach continuing to sour, unsure of where he was going.

"I thought I had everything figured out. I met Becca during freshman welcome week, and we were together from that moment on. I thought she was the one. Instead of going home to see my mom or visiting my dad, I went home with her on school breaks. I helped her dad build a shed for chrissakes!" Ethan slapped his forehead. "I called her parents Mom and Dad!"

"What happened?" Mable asked.

"To this day, I don't know what I did wrong."

Mable bit her lip. She had something to say, but she didn't want to say anything yet.

Ethan rubbed his stubble. "I thought things were fine once we started junior year. Becca seemed happy. I was busy keeping up with my honors classes while doing clinicals at a school so I was out the door by six a.m. most days and on top of that, I had to keep up with my class load and working in the library. I didn't have time for football games, movie nights, and parties like I had in previous years. I guess she just got bored?"

Mable spoke up, "We haven't known each other that long, but I can't imagine you did anything wrong—wait, you're not going to tell me you cheated on her, are you?"

Ethan chuckled and played with the drawstring on Mable's pajama top. "No, that's not me. Never."

Mable wiped her brow. "Phew, I mean I didn't think that was the case, but sometimes people can surprise you in the worst of ways."

"Tell me about it. That's how I feel about Becca sometimes."

"Did she cheat on you?"

"No. Well, honestly, I'm not a hundred percent sure. I hope not," Ethan said.

"So she just said, 'Hi Ethan, it's over?'"

"Basically. I guess to be fair, there were probably signs, but like I said, I had so much going on, I didn't realize she was unhappy until it was too late."

The room was dark, but a streetlight outside streamed in through the window so that Mable could see Ethan's face even through the dark shadows. He wasn't looking at her, and she knew he was replaying what had happened with his ex.

"After being at a school all day on Thursday, I'd rush over to the campus for two classes, I had a presentation at the six p.m. to nine p.m. class, and by the time I was dragging myself up the stairs to our second-floor apartment, I was ready to drop." He swallowed hard.

Mable reached out and took his hand. He lay down on the bed, so now he was on his back too. She looked down and smiled, seeing how Iggy was lying in the space below Ethan's feet. For her part, her feet were too close to the end of the bed to leave room for the small puppy.

"I walked into our apartment and turned on the kitchen light. Then I threw my backpack on a kitchen chair and rummaged in the fridge for something to eat. I made a turkey sandwich. Then I took my sandwich and walked into the living room. That's when I realized something was wrong. I looked at the walls and the pictures were gone." He laughed wryly and shook his head. "I legit thought that we'd gotten robbed, didn't even occur to me she'd left. I put down my sandwich on the coffee table and rushed into the bedroom. I was in a panic. What if she'd been there when we'd gotten robbed and was hurt? I was so dumb."

"I'm sorry this happened to you," Mable said.

"As you can guess, the bedroom was empty. Only my stuff was left, and that's when I ran to the bathroom and threw up."

"No turkey sandwiches, got it." That got a hint of a smile out of Ethan, and Mable felt that upturn of his lips all the way down to her toes.

"As I was sitting on our bed staring into our closet, my phone vibrated."

"Let me guess, that was her calling."

"Worse, she texted me. Just said it was over and to give her space."

"Oof. That's brutal."

"Tell me about it. We'd been together for over two years, and she couldn't be bothered to say it to my face. She coordinated getting and moving out all her stuff, and I had no clue what was happening." His voice cracked, and her heart ached for him.

"I'm so sorry. I don't know what to say." She reached out and ran her hand up and down his arm.

"After she was gone, I was in a dark place. I stopped going to class and called in to cancel going to work so much that they took me off the schedule. I wasn't eating. I slept a lot, but that was part the depression and part the Nyquil I was guzzling."

Mable turned to look at Ethan. "Nyquil?"

"When I was asleep, I wasn't thinking about Becca. It stopped my brain from asking over and over, What did I do wrong? What should I have done differently?"

She caressed his cheek. His eyes were glossy.

He took a ragged breath, and she took his hand and squeezed it. "It wasn't long before I was mixing Nyquil and booze. All I wanted to do was escape the pain, and generic Nyquil and cheap vodka seemed to do the trick. For a while at least."

"And your ex didn't check in?"

"No, but in hindsight, that was a good thing. If she had been talking to me, I think I would have driven myself nuts trying to win her back."

"You didn't have any good friends you could talk to?" Mable was having trouble understanding how Ethan had found himself so completely alone.

"I'd been with Becca from practically day one of college. All my friends were her friends too. When she ditched me, I think they either sided with her or felt like they didn't want to pick sides, so they must have stayed away from us both for a while. All I had were some people I was friendly acquaintances with—you know, people you see at school or work? Before now, if you didn't see me around for a while, would you think anything was wrong, or just that I was busy?"

"Honestly, I might not even think of you at all." She felt bad about saying that truth, and she gave him a squeeze to take away some of the sting of her words.

He hugged her back.

"I know exactly what you are saying, and it's true. There are plenty of people in our lives who are out of sight, out of mind. Not that you don't like them, it's just that they aren't your main friends, but they can become real friends at any point."

Mable rested her head again against Ethan's and kissed him. She pulled back and played with a curl on his forehead. He reached over and pushed a tendril of her hair back behind her ear.

Ethan began speaking again, and Mable could feel the tension in his body. She trailed her hand along his arm, offering a soothing touch.

"A couple of months into the breakup, a guy I knew pretty well, Joey, knocked on the door one day because I hadn't been to the class we were in for weeks. I didn't answer the door. I must have been totally out of it that day because the door wasn't locked. He pushed on it, it opened, and he came in to see if I was there. Later he told me he was shaking me and screaming in my face, but I wouldn't wake up. He told me he had nine-one-one on his phone and was about to hit send when I finally started mumbling."

"Sounds like you scared the crap out of him."

"He was pretty pissed, and I was a total jerk to him when I finally woke up all the way. Told him to get out and leave me alone."

"Did he?"

"Yes, and no. He left, but he called the university's mental health hotline."

Mable's eyes teared up, and she tried not to blink. Her throat was tight. She whispered. "I'm so glad he called."

"Me too. Even though most of me was mad, thinking he was invading my privacy, part of me was so grateful. I don't think I would have gotten help otherwise. I needed someone to intervene."

The hair on the back of Mable's neck stood up. "My entire life, I've always been surrounded by so many other people. You know, I come from a big family, and I've lived in Marley Creek all my life, so I know like everyone. When I was away at college, I went to Illinois State, and there were people from high school in literally all my classes. Even this summer in Germany, I went with a bunch of other Illinois State students. I can't imagine being alone like you were."

Ethan tucked a finger under her chin. "I hope you don't find out. It sucked. Thanks to Joey, I got some help and for once my dad being a total pain in the ass helped me. He threatened to go to the local TV stations and all the parent groups he could find on Facebook if they didn't let me withdraw from my classes with an incomplete."

"I mean, thank goodness for that. At least your GPA wasn't destroyed."

Ethan played with Mable's hair, and she closed her eyes. "I lost my housing, of course, and I had to move back in with my dad."

"How did you wind up in Marley Creek instead of staying with your dad?"

Ethan cleared his throat, his voice hard. "Dad's current wife and I don't get along."

Mable wasn't sure what to say, and she was having trouble keeping her eyes open, so she said, "I see."

She could feel him relax into the mattress. She tried to stifle a yawn, but it was no use.

"I've unloaded enough of my trauma on you for one evening. How about I be the big spoon and we get some sleep?"

"That sounds amazing." She turned on her side and scooched her butt, so it was pressing against him. He rolled onto his side, cuddling her, and put his arm over her. It was as if he were her own personal thundershirt. She drifted off to sleep as he kissed her lightly where her shoulder met her neck.

Chapter Seventeen

♥

Even though he had nowhere to be and was in bed with a beautiful woman, his internal alarm clock still had him out of bed and in the kitchen, trying to remember how to make that French press coffee by seven a.m. Iggy ran around his feet, distracting him, and he gave up on the coffee and decided to take Iggy for a walk. He wrangled Iggy into her harness and clipped on the lead.

A block into the walk, sweat was running down his back. It was going to be a hot one. He turned onto Main Street and wished he'd brought some water and a collapsible bowl for Iggy. He made a note to check and see if Sean and Nicole had already gotten a collapsible bowl or if he should see if they sold any at Pupcakes and Clawssants this afternoon. The pet bakery usually had a decent stock of pet supplies, and it was only another block down Main Street. He might as well head over there, and maybe he'd be able to see in the storefront if they had bowls and if he was really lucky, thundershirts as well.

Iggy trotted along, her little pink tongue hanging out. It only took a few minutes before they were in front of Marley Creek's second most popular bakery. Since it wasn't even eight in the morning yet, Ethan was surprised to see the open sign and activity in the bakery. Kate Sterling waved at Ethan, so he opened the door and walked in. The door shut behind him, and he felt his back pocket to make sure he'd brought his wallet. He had.

Kate was about the same height as Mable, but she was stockier. She was wearing a sleeveless T-shirt, and Ethan appreciated how cut her arms were. He'd have to ask her what gym she went to. Her short blonde hair had green tips this month.

"Hey, Ethan! Who's that you have with you?"

"This is Iggy."

Iggy was tugging on the leash, trying to get Ethan to let her sniff each and every single thing in the store. Next to the front door of the store was a welcome mat with a couple of dog bowls of water sitting out. A little sign said, "For the Pups." Ethan guided Iggy over to the water, and she quickly started lapping it up.

"Don't tell me our mayor got a puppy?" Kate asked excitedly.

"No, this is Sean and Nicole's dog. I'm not sure if you know them?"

"I don't think I do, but hopefully I will get to know them now that they have Iggy."

"Sean's my half-brother. He owns Jesse's Pub, and Nicole is his wife."

"I've been to Jesse's Pub a few times, great food. Is he the big guy with the brown hair and a scruffy face?"

Ethan chuckled, "Yes, that's him."

"Are you dog-sitting then?"

"Actually, I'm helping a friend. She's dog-sitting for Sean and Nicole. I don't know if you know her? Mable Weaverton?"

Kate shook her head. "No, I don't, but that last name sounds familiar."

"She's from a big family. Maybe you've run into someone else from her family."

"Could be. I'm still new to Marley Creek. What kind of diet is Iggy on? Can they have a regular treat, or do you need a grain-free one? I've got peanut butter and banana."

"As far as I know, she doesn't need to avoid grains, but we might as well be on the safe side and go with the grain-free."

Kate put on a pair of gloves and picked up a doggy treat in the shape of a shamrock. She moved around the bakery case and over to Iggy. "Hey puppy, would you like a treat?"

Iggy gave a little yip and wagged her tail. Kate knelt down and looked at Ethan. "Have you tried to teach her to sit yet?"

"Not really. You want to give it a try?"

"I'd love to."

Kate made eye contact with Iggy. "Sit."

Iggy barked.

"Sit."

Iggy pawed at the ground.

Kate dropped her voice, "Sit."

Iggy sat. Kate gave the treat to Iggy. Iggy put it daintily in her mouth and then dropped it to the floor, sniffed it, and gobbled it up.

Kate stood back up and took off the gloves. "She's got quite a personality!"

"She's a handful! That's why I'm helping Mable out."

"Oh, hey, speaking of helping. What are y'all doing tomorrow night?"

"I don't have anything going on, but I can't speak for Mable. What's up?"

"The pet parade is on Saturday, and I'm trying to get a float together. Any chance you two can help me out?"

"What are we talking about?" Ethan said.

"I have a pickup truck that I borrowed from a friend. I could really use some help decorating it. The landlord here let me put the truck in the garage behind the building, and I've got a pile of crafty supplies and posterboard in the back. I just need people."

"I'm not artistic, but I am enthusiastic."

Kate grinned. "I can offer pizza and beer as payment."

"Now we're talking. I'll check with Mable, but just know she's working on an extensive project for school, so she might be a no."

Kate nodded. "I understand. I appreciate you even thinking about helping. And if you guys want, you could sit in the truck's bed with Iggy during the parade. Would you want to be in the parade?"

Ethan scrunched up his face in thought. "That sounds like fun. I'll see what Mable has going on and if she's up for it."

Kate grinned, "Thank you so much! I've only been open a few months and I need to get the word out to more people!"

Ethan smiled, "If half the dogs in town like the treats as much as Iggy, you'll be in business for years to come."

Kate's eyes light up, "From your lips to the Universe's ears. Now, is there anything else I can help you with today?"

"Any chance you carry tiny thundershirts? Iggy was a total wreck when we had that storm the other night."

Kate, "I'm pretty sure I have one small enough to fit her. Let's take a look."

Kate led Ethan over to a rack filled with little doggie outfits, harnesses, and thundershirts. She looked down at Iggy, "How old is she?"

"I'm not exactly sure, but I'd say less than six months?"

Kate pulled a tiny shirt off the rack. "The extra-extra small goes up to eight pounds." She handed it to Ethan.

"This looks perfect. I'll take it."

"Great, I'll ring you up."

"Give me a dozen of the grain-free treats as well."

Kate processed Ethan's card and put the treats and shirt in a recycled paper bag with the store's logo on it.

"If you have a business card, put it in the bag so I can give it to Sean and Nicole. I'm sure they'll be one of your biggest customers."

"Awesome, thank you so much!" Kate smiled and handed Ethan the bag. "And let me know if you can make it on Friday!"

Ethan held up the bag. "Just call the number on the card?"

Kate nodded, "Perfect."

"Say goodbye, Iggy."

"It was great to meet you, Iggy," Kate said.

Ethan walked back toward Sean and Nicole's with a happy, hydrated puppy by his side.

Chapter Eighteen

♥

Mable watched as Ethan tried to get Iggy into the thundershirt. "Maybe you should just try to put it on her later, when she's less excited."

"We've been with her for what, four days now, and has she ever not been excited?"

Mable nodded. "You got me there; she's full of energy all the time."

"Except—"

"When *Bluey* is on!" Mable finished his thought. It gave her a warm fuzzy feeling, knowing they were on the same wavelength.

Ethan backed away from Iggy and picked up the remote. Iggy was barking and running around in a circle, chasing her own tail. As soon as the opening notes of the theme song played, Iggy stopped chasing her tail, sat down, and put her head on her paws.

Mable gasped. "That's amazing. *Bluey* is totally pavlov-ing her!"

"Pavloving her?" Ethan raised an eyebrow.

"You know what I mean."

Ethan nodded and quickly put on Iggy's thundershirt. "It fits on the tightest setting for now."

Mable went into the kitchen and brought them each a mug of coffee. Ethan had taken off the thundershirt and was sitting on the couch holding a business card and his phone. "Coffee?" she asked.

"Thank you." He took the warm mug from her, and their hands brushed. She sat down on the couch right next to him and leaned over his shoulder. "Whatcha doing?"

"It's Kate's info." He kept typing.

"Kate?"

"Kate, the owner of the pet bakery, Pupcakes and Clawssants."

Mable nodded.

Ethan put his phone down and gave her his full attention. "She asked if we could help her with something."

"What's going on?"

Ethan put his free arm around Mable, and she snuggled in closer. Not that she had much experience with dating, but in the little dating that she did, she'd never felt comfortable enough to feel this relaxed sitting next to a man.

"Kate needs help decorating her truck for the pet parade, so she asked if we'd be interested in helping her Friday night. I know the main goal right now is to get your project done. Do you think you'll have enough completed by tomorrow night to take a break? Just for the evening?"

Mable bit her bottom lip, her brows knit together. "I don't know Ethan, I want to, but."

Ethan reached for her hand. "It's okay, I get it. The work has to come first. What if we play it by ear? I'll tell Kate I'm definitely in, and you may be with me?"

Tension left her body. "Let's do that."

"Great, I'll give Kate a call in a little while and let her know. Now, what have you got planned for today? How can I help?"

Mable gave Ethan an update on the progress of her project, and she was so happy that he didn't pick up his phone while she was talking. He even asked some excellent questions that helped her plan a few aspects of the second half of the paper. Best of all, he offered to take Iggy out for the afternoon so she would have complete peace for a few hours.

She made good use of the time and was finishing up the rough draft of her paper by five p.m. Just as she was finishing her closing paragraph, her phone vibrated, and she saw the name of her mentor, Susan Brown, pop up.

She hit save on her document and answered Susan's call.

"Hi Mable, it's Susan calling to check in."

"It's so nice to hear from you, Susan!"

"I thought I'd try to connect with you, since we are less than two weeks out from the start of the school year. How are you feeling about your upcoming internship?"

"I've been so busy working on my summation project for the study abroad program that I haven't had time to think about working at Ida B. Wells Elementary this fall."

"Mm-hmm," Susan said, "How's the project going? Are you avoiding procrastination perfection?"

Mable pictured Susan sitting behind her desk, her thick hair in a chignon complete with two pencils, most likely wearing a classic Ralph Lauren professorial outfit. She assumed Susan had always completed her assignments well before they were due and never looked down to find that her white shirt had a big blob of jelly on it. Mable pulled the top of her shirt up to her mouth and sucked off the jelly before answering Susan.

"Actually, I was finishing the last paragraph of the rough draft, as you called."

"Look at you!" Susan said. "You're ahead of schedule! Everything needs to be submitted before August nineteenth, correct?"

"Yes, I've been planning to have it in on the eighteenth."

"That gives you ten days, more than enough time, I think." The sound of nails tapping in the background helped Mable picture Susan more clearly. She knew that was a habit Susan had when she was thinking.

"How are you feeling about your schedule?"

"Since I'm on the phone with you, can I get some feedback?" Mable asked.

"Of course, that's what I'm here for."

"I've been asked if I can help with a parade float tomorrow."

"A float? Oh, that's right, the pet parade is always a week or so before school goes back into session."

"How did you?" Mable started, then recalled, "I always forget you grew up near Marley Creek. I just think of you at Illinois State."

"Very understandable, but now you might run into me at the grocery store this fall. I'm moving back to Marley Creek in a few weeks."

Mable grinned, "I know we will run into each other. Marley Creek is still super small. Are you sure you're ready for that?"

"Well, it can't be helped, I'm moving back to take care of a family member."

Mable was quiet, unsure of what to say.

"But let's get back to you, so you're thinking of taking a break tomorrow night?"

"Um, yes, but I'm worried," Mable said.

"Why is that?"

"I'm worried this is just me procrastinating."

Mable heard the nail tapping again and was relieved. She knew this meant Susan was taking her concerns to heart and would offer some helpful advice. "Do you have your planner handy?"

"Sure, I use the calendar function on my laptop."

"Great, let's look at what you need to do and how many days you have left," Susan said.

They spent the next ten minutes working on Mable's schedule, and by the time they were done, not only did she have time to help with the float, she also had enough time that she could afford to take most of Saturday off as well.

"How are you feeling about things now?" Susan asked.

"I can't believe I'm saying this, but now that I have a plan to finish the project, I'm energized. Once we hang up, I'm going to set aside the paper to review and revise tomorrow, and tonight I'm going to work for a couple of hours on the video component."

"Just what a mentor wants to hear," Susan said.

"Thank you so much for your help."

"Enjoy your Friday night and the parade!"

"Will I see you there?" Mable said.

"I wish I could, but I've got to finish a few things around the condo. The realtor is coming to take pictures on Saturday."

"Wow, so you're making a permanent move to Marley Creek."

"Pretty much."

Mable could hear the tension in her mentor's voice, and her chest tightened. She didn't know the details, but it sounded like Susan was going through a tough time and she still had the bandwidth to help Mable.

"I hope everything goes smoothly."

"Thanks so much, Mable. Would you like me to check in with you next week, or do you think you've got this?"

"I think I've got this, but if it's okay with you, can I email you if things change?"

"Please do!"

"Great, it's a plan. Thanks again," Mable said.

"You're most welcome."

Susan ended the call, and Mable put down her phone. Then she picked it up and sent a quick text message to Ethan.

MABLE: Tell Kate I'm in to decorate tomorrow!

ETHAN: (high five emoji) (celebrate emoji)

MABLE: Now I just need to put in about three more hours of work tonight and about five or six tomorrow.

ETHAN: You got this!

Still feeling energized from her call with Susan and the beacon of support she'd found in Ethan, Mable finished the last few sentences of her paper and then moved on to start work on the video presentation.

Chapter Nineteen

♥

Ethan sat in one of the little bistro chairs Sean and Nicole had on their front porch and waited for Mable to come out. Iggy was snapped into her lead and was enjoying the smells to be found in the front yard. She climbed between the hosta plants, and then when she heard Mable shutting the front door, she pranced onto the walkway. Mable locked the door and put the key ring in her pocket. She turned around and Iggy yipped, excited to get going.

"Are you sure Kate won't mind that we are bringing Iggy?"

"Kate runs a pet bakery; she'd probably mind if we didn't bring Miss Iggy," Ethan said.

"You're right, I'm being silly."

Ethan playfully bumped into Mable. "I love that you are so considerate of others." He looked at Mable's profile, admiring her long eyelashes and the swoop of her nose. They walked together in tandem down the block and then over to Main Street.

"This is your first Marley Creek Pet Parade, right?" Mable asked.

"Yep, anything I need to know?"

"I feel like if you've seen one small-town parade, you've seen them all. As long as our float isn't behind the fire trucks or the horses, we'll be fine."

Ethan crossed his fingers. They arrived at Pupcakes and Clawssants, and Kate was at the door, ready to welcome them in. Today she had her short hair dyed in the shades of a rainbow.

"Your hair is so cute! Is that permanent?" Mable asked.

Kate brushed her hand over the top of her spiky hair. "Semi, I should get about 10 washes out of it before it fades away."

"Very cool," Ethan said.

"I thought it would be fun for the parade," Kate said.

Ethan put his hand on Mable's lower back. "Kate, this is my, ah..." His stomach clenched as he panicked, unsure what to call Mable. She was much more than a friend, but they hadn't had a relationship discussion.

"Hi, I'm Mable, Ethan's good friend." She put out her hand, and Kate shook it.

"Nice to meet you, Mable," Kate let go of Mable's hand and continued. "Ethan said you are in the middle of a big project for college. I really appreciate you coming out to help me tonight."

"I've gone to the pet parade since I was a kid, but this will be the first time that I'm helping to decorate a float."

Kate pointed with her thumb over her shoulder toward two long tables that were laden with all sorts of markers from Sharpies to puffy paint and a pile of poster boards, stencils, construction paper, silk flowers, and glue guns. "I've got everything I could think of that we might need to decorate. I didn't realize there was a parade until I went to the Marley Creek Business Association meeting on the first. I'm sorry this is so last minute."

Ethan smiled reassuringly. "We've got this. Between Mable and me, we've done our share of decorating and crafting."

"I have five younger siblings, and I'm working on becoming a school psychologist. I know my way around a set of markers and a glue gun," Mable said.

"I've got to tell you; I want to hug you both so much right now!" Kate said.

Ethan looked at Mable and raised an eyebrow. She nodded in return.

"Group hug!" Ethan said, and they both embraced Kate.

When they moved away. Ethan noticed that Kate's eyes were glossy. He didn't want to comment on her sudden emotion, afraid it might embarrass her, so he said, "Do you have a theme for the float?"

Kate pointed to her head. "I thought we'd go with the colors of the rainbow and maybe something like treats for all your pets?"

"Mable, do you have any artistic skills?"

Mable laughed. The sound of it made warmth spread through him. Not only did she laugh often, but she was also never afraid to laugh at herself. Becca had never been much for laughing. She'd said she hated the sound of her own laugh.

"Gosh, no, I can't even draw stick figures well, but I am good at using stencils."

"Perfect," Kate said.

Kate and Mable walked over to the tables. Ethan took Iggy off the leash and she ran right over to the water bowls Kate had put out. Then Ethan walked over to where Kate and Mable were making poster boards. It wasn't long before they had a system where Mable stenciled the sign, then she passed it over to Ethan who drew various caricatures of cats, dogs, and other pets, and then lastly to Kate who added flowers and other flourishes with the glue gun.

"I think I've burned all my fingers with this glue gun," Kate said.

"Ouch, hot glue is the worst," Mable said. "Should we take a break?"

Kate looked at the display of drying signs they'd made and then at her watch. "I think it's time for a break. I've got cola, water, and some beer in the fridge. What do you two like on your pizza?"

Ethan leaned back in his chair. He didn't care what was on the pizza; he'd be fine with whatever Mable chose. He realized that at this moment; he felt better than he could remember. For the first time in ages, he was having fun, and he didn't have a constant worry about Mable leaving him. The scars left by Becca weren't coloring his time with Mable. This must be the key to dating. All he had to do was not fall for Mable, and he'd be happy.

Mable looked over at Ethan. "Pepperoni is my favorite. Is that okay with you?"

"Sure, sounds great." He smiled. It was so good to be around her. He wouldn't mind if this night never ended.

Mable tossed her hair over her shoulder, and she was close enough that Ethan caught some of the ends and then let the silky strands go. She turned to him and put her hand on his thigh. He was so glad he'd chosen to go with shorts. The heat of her palm on his leg made him struggle not to slide her hand up further until she was cupping him. Hopefully, that would happen later once they were back at the house.

"Pepperoni, it is," said Kate. "I'll call Best Pizza Near Me." Kate dialed the phone and made the order.

"I can walk over and pick it up." Mable said.

"Are you sure?" Kate said.

"Yes, Iggy could use a little walk. I'll take her with," Mable said.

"Do you want me to go with you?" Ethan said.

"No, that's fine. You hang out here with Kate. I won't be long."

Ethan nodded and waited to see if his stomach clenched with upset because Mable didn't want him to come along to get the pizza. He looked down in disbelief, not a twinge of anxiety that Mable might be mad at him. When Becca hadn't wanted him around, he'd felt like he was about to have an ulcer.

"The pizza will be ready in half an hour," Kate said. "In the meantime, want to see the truck?"

"I'd love to check it out!" Ethan said.

Kate got up and walked to her back room. She pulled out a couple of beers and offered one to Ethan.

Ethan took the beer and twisted off the top.

"Did you want one too, Mable?" Kate asked.

"I'll have one when I get back with the pizza."

Kate made sure the glue gun was off, and then she got the keys to the store. "If you want to lock the front door for me and put Iggy on her leash, we can leave from the back and I can show you the truck. Then, Mable, you can head over to Best Pizza Near Me from there."

"Perfect," Mable said.

Ethan put Iggy's leash back on her and gave her a few pets while Mable locked the door. He felt such a lightness in his step working together with Mable. He felt so in sync with her. When he'd been with Becca, it had been about making sure he knew her moods, but this was completely different. He didn't need to be ready to soothe or calm Mable because he'd made a mistake or said the wrong thing. She seemed happy just to have him around.

Chapter Twenty

♥

Mable put in her headphones and called Hannah as soon as she was out of Ethan's earshot. "What's up?" Hannah said.

"Are you busy? Please tell me you aren't."

"It's a Friday night in Marley Creek. I'm at home eating popcorn and re-watching *Bridgerton.*"

"Again?"

"You are so rude. I can't help it. I have a crush on Eloise and Colin."

"Maybe you need to get back out there and date someone."

"Mab, are you serious right now?"

"Spending time with Ethan has been enlightening. Now I want everyone out there coupling up."

"Oh my God, are you two a couple now?!?" Hannah squealed.

"Not in so many words, but I kind of feel like yes, and I like it?"

"Shut up! I'm so happy for you!"

"I'm grinning so hard my face hurts. But that's not exactly why I called. I mean, yes, it kind of is, but also, I want to do it."

"Do what?"

Mable rolled her eyes. "Have sex with Ethan."

"Whattt?!?" Hannah screamed into the phone so loud that Iggy yipped.

"You are freaking out, the dog. I think you broke my eardrum."

"How could I not yell, and that's why you have two ears," Hannah said.

"So, what do you think? Is it crazy? We have only been hanging out for like a week."

"More like you've known him for months, you've known his older brother for years, and y'all have been living together for the past week."

"When you put it like that, it sounds much better," Mable said.

"Good, I say go for it. If that is what you want to do and Ethan is down for it, have all the sex."

"Thanks for your permission, bestie."

"You're welcome. Anything else I can help you with?" Hannah said.

"This conversation isn't exactly going how I thought it would go. I was expecting to have a talk about why I was making the decision to have sex with Ethan."

"I'm guessing it's because you two have some amazing chemistry and can't keep your hands off each other?"

"Well, that's part of it."

"And he makes you feel safe enough that you can tell him what you need," Hannah said.

"Yes, that too."

"Fabulous! Why are we still talking? Why aren't you dragging that man off to bed?"

"Because we are at Pupcakes and Clawssants helping the owner Kate with her parade float," Mable said.

"Her name is Kate? I've passed by there on my way to work. She's got the short, funky dyed hair, right?"

"Yep, today it's rainbow-colored," Mable said.

"She's got such amazing bone structure; she can pull it off. And she has those pouty lips…"

"Hmm, sounds like you have a crush besides the *Bridgerton* crew."

"I don't even know if she's single or who all she dates," Kate said.

"Do you want me to find out?"

"No! You need to be concentrating on a wild night with Ethan."

"Once we get home," Mable said.

"Ah, I am so excited for you!"

"Any words of wisdom?"

"That's a great question. I would say don't think about it too much, but I feel like you've been overthinking sex for a long time now," Hannah said.

"It seems so invasive," Mable said.

"True, you do literally have to let him in," Hannah said.

Mable bit her bottom lip. "Thinking about letting Ethan in, it doesn't scare me."

"Sounds like you are ready, my friend," Hannah said.

Mable stood outside Best Pizza Near Me.

"See, we've had the talk. I have clarity about my why."

"Now you're taking all the sexy out of the sex talk."

Mable chuckled. "For real, thanks so much, Hannah. I'd be a mess without you."

"I love you too, girlie." Hannah said and made kissy noises into the phone.

"Ew, it's like you are inside my ear," Mable said.

"Call me and tell me all about it. Or not! Whatever works."

"Love you, Hannah."

"Byyyyyeeee!"

Hannah ended the call. Mable put her phone in her back pocket and walked into the restaurant.

***

After sharing pizza, drinking a couple of beers and more crafting, they were finally on their way back to the house. Even though it was still very humid out, a pleasant breeze was blowing as they walked. Mable put her arm in Ethan's free arm. The breeze was making her a little chilly.

"Are you sure you can take time out for the parade tomorrow?" Ethan asked.

"Yes, I talked with my mentor, and she agreed that I'm in a good place for a quick break. But then I've got to get right back to it tomorrow afternoon."

"You got this," Ethan said.

Mable smiled. With each moment they spent together tonight, her decision to have sex for the first time was solidified. They walked up the step to the front door, and Mable unlocked it.

"I'll put on *Bluey* for Iggy," Ethan said.

Butterflies fluttered in Mable's stomach. She bit her lip. "Ethan?"

"What's up?" He was looking down at the remote while Iggy ran around between his legs.

"I was thinking," she said.

The TV show theme song played in the background as Ethan put down the remote and gave Mable his full attention. Iggy pawed the carpet and then made a couple of circles before she lay down with her head on her paws.

Mable worried her lip. Was she sure she wanted to do this? She looked at Ethan, his thick, dark hair curling a little at the ends and his broad shoulders, and the way she knew how cut he was under his T-shirt. All she wanted was to run her hands down his chest and then pull him on top of her. She needed the weight of him on top of her like Iggy needed that thundershirt.

"Everything okay?" Ethan said.

"It's more than okay." Mable walked over to Ethan. She bent down and touched her lips to his, softly kissing him. He pulled her to him and deepened the kiss. Mable felt warmth low in her belly and she pushed her tongue into his mouth, wanting more of him now. She felt his cock hard against her stomach, and it made her more aroused. This was the right choice. Mable broke off the kiss and put her forehead against his.

"God, you're so hot," Ethan said.

The scent of him filled her nose and put her want into overdrive. She tried to catch her breath. "Ethan, I've changed my mind."

He froze and pulled back. He started to take a step back from her, and she grabbed his hand, tugging him back to her. "Wait, let me finish, please."

He stopped and waited.

"I'm trying to say I changed my mind about not wanting to have sex. I want to, with you."

He wrapped her in his arms. "Are you sure? We don't have to. I'm happy just being in the same room as you. I'd be happy if we sat on the couch and held hands all night."

His eyes burned bright, and she knew to the tips of her toes that he was sincere. "I'm sure. As long as you want to, of course."

The butterflies had taken flight and been replaced by heat and desire. Her panties were soaked the moment he said he'd be happy to hold hands with her. "Before we do this, there is just one thing. I am on the pill. I've been on it for ages, but you still need to wear a condom."

Ethan blushed. "Actually, I have a box of them in my bag."

Mable put her hands on her hips. "That's pretty bold of you."

Ethan waved his hands. "It's not that, I swear! They've been in my bag for probably a year. I took them on a trip with Becca and never took the open box out."

Mable frowned. "I'm sorry I said anything. I didn't mean to bring up your ex."

"She's the last person I want to be talking about or thinking about right now."

"The other thing is," Mable paused, and even though there was nothing to be embarrassed about, she still felt her face heat as she said it. "I'm a virgin."

"You're what?"

Mable fanned her face, "Just technically. I haven't had sex sex. Oral, yes, and I have a toy. I know how to take care of myself.

But I've never had like full-on intercourse." She looked down, "I'm sorry, now you're blushing too."

"Don't be sorry. I'm honored that you feel like I'm worth having sex with," Ethan said.

Mable's eyes got watery. "You're gonna make me cry."

Ethan wagged his eyebrows. "Hopefully soon I'll be making you cry out my name."

Mable burst out laughing. "I needed that. Let's go," she said and led him to the bedroom.

Chapter Twenty-One

♥

Ethan finished showering and put on a pair of shorts. As he brushed his teeth, he thought about what had just happened with Mable. He'd never been anyone's first experience with sex. He'd learned and savored all the moans, sighs, and quivers she'd made when he'd gone down on her the other day. When they'd had sex last night, she'd been more subdued. "That can't be good," he said to himself. They'd laid together afterward. She'd cuddled against him, and she acted content in every way possible. But he had to face it. The sex was not as good for her as it was for him. Maybe he should have gone slower or tried to last longer, or maybe it was normal for her not to have an orgasm.

He finished brushing his teeth and went back into the bedroom. Mable wasn't there. He left the guest bedroom and walked down the hall toward the living room. In the living room, Mable was sitting on the couch with Iggy on her lap. The TV was on, but the volume was muted. The light from the TV shone on Mable's face, and it took his breath away. He would never tire of this girl. "I l-l," he started to say and then stopped himself. He could not be in love with her. That would ruin everything. He cleared his throat. "Is Iggy sleeping?"

Mable nodded and patted the cushion next to her. Ethan quietly lowered himself down, trying not to jostle the sleeping puppy. "Everything okay?" He asked, his throat tightening with worry.

"I wanted to tell you why I was still a virgin," she whispered.

"You don't have to explain anything to me," he said.

"Thank you, but I want to. You know how I'm the oldest of six kids?"

Ethan nodded, even though he was fairly certain she was asking rhetorically. He laced his hand into hers. Her hand was moist. She must be nervous. He wished he knew how to reassure her that whatever reasons she had to be hesitant around sex were perfectly acceptable.

She took a deep breath and blew it out through her mouth. "I was an oops baby. My mom got pregnant halfway through college, even though she was on the pill. She'd been dating my dad for over a year; they decided to get married, and as you can guess, she dropped out of school. They had me, and a couple of years after me, my brother, then eighteen months later, another brother. And so on. My dad is a semi-truck driver, and he is long haul, so he's only home a couple of days a week."

"That must have been tough on your mom, and you kids, of course."

"When I was growing up, it was hard to see her side of things. She was just the parent who was always tired and rarely had the energy or time to come to my events."

"I'm sorry." Ethan didn't grow up with any brothers or sisters in the same house, so he couldn't relate to her experience, but he wanted her to know he was listening.

"By the time I was ten, I had been hearing for years how she'd dropped out of college and given up on her dreams because of me. She'd loved science, and she'd been going to school to become a chemist."

"I'm sure she could have gone back to school; she could have put you all in daycare."

"I guess, but it would have been really expensive."

"You're right. I didn't think of that. Boy, that sucks."

"When I was a teenager, my mom relied on me to watch my younger brothers and sister. It's kind of crazy that I want to get into education considering how much time I spent helping raise them. You'd think the last thing I'd want to do was voluntarily spend my days with other people's kids."

"I think your life experiences are going to help you in your career."

"Thank you, baby." She squeezed his hand.

His heart sped up. She'd called him baby; she'd never called him that before.

"When I was in eighth grade, I had a huge crush on a boy. I had a phone by then on the condition that my mom knew my password. So, me and this boy were texting back and forth. Nothing serious at all, but my mom saw the texts, and she freaked out. She told me the worst thing I could do was to have sex—sex destroyed dreams."

"Sex destroyed dreams. That's heavy stuff for an eighth grader."

"Tell me about it. Gosh, just talking about it brings me right back there. Her face was white as a sheet." Mable let go of his hand. She wrapped her hand around his bicep. "My mom put her hands on my arms so tight, I thought I was going to have bruises." She squeezed his arm as she spoke.

He patted her hand, and she let go and put her hand back in his. Her hand wasn't clammy anymore. He rubbed her palm with his thumb.

"Then I got a little older and went on the pill, just in case. But anytime I got close to a guy," She shrugged. "I just didn't want to risk it. How could I trust I wouldn't wind up like my mom? She wasn't trying to get pregnant, and she took birth control, and she still lost her dreams. During undergrad, I found myself not even interested in dating, especially when I came back to school after winter or summer break. Coming home was showing me what could happen if I screwed up." Tears were swimming in Mable's eyes.

Ethan wished he'd put a shirt on now so he could at least use his shirt to wipe away her tears. He reached over and used his thumb to brush away her tears.

"I'm happy you shared all of this with me, but I feel awful that you've felt for so long that sex is a dream killer."

"Thank you," she sniffed.

"If something were to happen, we have options. Any way you look at it, you're not going to live your mother's life."

Mable was taking shaking breaths. Iggy woke up and hopped down off her lap onto the floor. Ethan pulled Mable onto his lap and put her head against his shoulder. Her breathing was still rough, so he rubbed her back, making soothing circles. After a few minutes, he felt Mable relax in his arms. "Mable, are you falling asleep?" he asked.

"Mm-hmm," she said.

He gave her a hug.

"Ethan, I really like you."

Ethan felt as if she'd reached in and petted his nervous heart. He wanted so much more, but that wouldn't be good for him. "I like you too," he replied. Keeping it to *like* was safe. His lids were heavy, and the weight of her on him was cozy. What could be better than falling asleep with a beautiful girl who trusted him in his arms?

Chapter Twenty -Two

♥

Mable was in the middle of a dream about Ethan. He was kissing her ear and making little growling noises. As she slowly came awake, she realized she was on the couch and Iggy was licking her face. "Blech," she said. She sat up fully and wiped her ear with the sleeve of her T-shirt. Ethan was asleep on the recliner near her. She was surprised he hadn't gone to sleep in the bedroom instead of staying by her. Her heart swelled. He was such a good guy.

The actual sex had been okay. Of course, she hadn't known what to expect. She probably should have researched it because she was sure it could have been better. She went into the kitchen and began to make some coffee. The clock on the stove said it was already a quarter past eight, and they needed to meet up at Kate's place by nine-fifteen. Mable was planning to put a little braid in Iggy's hair, and she didn't know how long it would take to get the dog to sit still long enough for a braid.

Ethan made a little snoring sound, and Mable looked over at him. She'd unloaded on him last night, and even after all that, he'd said he liked her. Her legs staggered as a realization hit her. She didn't just like him. She was falling in love with him. Her heart sped up. Should she tell him? She'd never been in this situation before, but she knew he'd been deeply in love with Becca. Was he truly over his ex? Everything she'd seen, and he'd said, seemed to show that he was in a good place and had moved on. She hoped her instincts were right; otherwise, she might wind up heartbroken.

Mable shook herself; she was tired of being guarded. She'd taken a big step last night, and she wasn't going to look for something that made her regret her choice. Ethan was a great guy, and he was here with her now when he didn't have to be here at all. In the beginning, he was here for Iggy, but that had changed, and now he was here for her. Later today, after the parade, she'd talk to him about their future. She was certain she wanted to see him once Sean and Nicole came back, and she knew he must feel the same way. It would be tough with him being a live-in manny for Franklin and Liam and her having classes on top of the year-long internship, but she believed with some planning, they could make time for each other.

She felt light as a feather as she poured each of them a cup of coffee. She set the cups on the table. Mable took out the toaster. She opened the refrigerator and took out the leftover sourdough bread they had from Donnie's as well as some natural peanut butter and the regular butter Ethan liked to add to his coffee, and set it all on the counter.

It felt good to prepare a meal for someone she might love. Sure, it wasn't much of a meal, but she wasn't much of a cook.

She put a couple of plates, napkins, and silverware on the table. Mable got out Iggy's food, and Iggy ran over and started barking before she could open the package and dole out her morning portion. The barking woke Ethan up, who stretched awake with a loud groan.

"Good morning, sleepyhead," she said in a sing-song voice.

"Hey, you," he said.

Mable's heart stopped for a second as she took in his adorable bedhead and sculpted chest. He stood and stretched. Her mouth went dry as her eyes traced his abs and that little happy trail of hair on his lower abdomen. She was still a little sore, but maybe later they could try the whole sex thing again.

"I sort of made breakfast."

"Oh, yeah?"

"I took out the toaster and some bread, plus stuff you can spread on it."

"I'm going to have to start laying off the carbs." He patted his completely flat stomach.

Mable snorted. "Please, you could grate cheese with those abs." She walked over to him and ran her hand over his stomach. "We could work out later?"

"What did you have in mind?"

She licked her lips. "Some major bedroom cardio."

"I'm in." He pulled her to him and smashed his lips against hers. She felt tingles all over.

Iggy circled them as they kissed, yipping.

Ethan broke off the kiss and attempted to adjust his shorts. Mable felt a burst of pride. She'd made him feel like that.

"I think Iggy needs to go outside," he said.

She walked over to the table and picked up a cup of coffee. "Take your coffee with so it doesn't get cold."

"Good thinking. What time is it?"

Mable looked back at the stove. "Crap, it's almost eight forty-five. We've only got half an hour before we have to leave!"

"No worries, you go ahead and shower. I only need a few minutes to clean up. I can help brush Iggy while you get ready."

She wrapped her arms around his neck and gave him a quick kiss on the cheek. "You're the best."

She watched the tips of his ears redden as he ducked his head and walked Iggy to the back door. Then she gulped down most of her coffee and went to take a shower.

At exactly nine-fifteen, they were locking the front door. "I'm so glad that we have nice weather for the parade today," Mable said.

"Finally, the humidity isn't almost a hundred percent!" Ethan looked up at the sky. "There isn't a cloud in the sky."

Mable looked up as well. "Nothing but blue skies," she said. They turned the corner onto Main Street, and even though the parade wouldn't begin for a couple more hours, people had already placed folding chairs along the street to save their spots. The corners of Mable's mouth turned up. "When I was a kid, we'd all wear our new school backpacks—well, I always had a new one and the younger kids mostly had hand-me-downs—and we'd fill those bags with a ridiculous amount of candy from the parade."

"I wonder how that tradition got started. I totally forgot floats give out candy to kids. We should have checked with Kate to see if she needed us to bring candy," Ethan said.

"Oh no, I hope she didn't forget candy for the parade. Kids can get mean when you're not throwing candy at them."

"You're kidding," Ethan said.

"I'm exaggerating"—she put her thumb and forefinger close together—"this much."

"Yikes!" Ethan laughed.

She put her arm in his, and they continued walking to Kate's store.

As they passed New Age Stones and Witch Crafts, Mable heard someone call her name. She turned around, and Hannah ran up to her and Ethan.

Hannah had her red hair in two braids, and she was wearing a T-shirt with the store logo and a pair of khaki capris. She was smiling so widely Mable could count all her teeth.

"Hey, girl! What's going on?" Hannah gave Mable a big hug and whispered in her ear. "Did you do the deed?"

Mable whispered back, "Shush, we'll talk later."

Hannah stepped back.

"Hi Hannah, nice to see you," Ethan said.

Hannah gave Ethan the once-over and said, "You're looking good, Ethan. Are you having a very relaxing summer?"

Mable elbowed her friend in the ribs.

"It's been pretty great. I've gotten to spend time with Iggy here, and Mable, of course." His eyes fixed on Mable.

Hannah gave Mable a knowing look. Mable wasn't sure exactly what the knowing look was, but she figured Hannah would tell her all about it when they caught up later.

"Did I hear y'all are going to be on the float for the pet bakery?"

"Yep, we'll be in the back of the pickup truck. Do you want to join us? I'm sure there's room," Ethan said.

"Man, I would love to, but Zaina is paying me to hang out here and give flyers out for our upcoming essential oil workshops. She's doing a big back-to-school thing for teachers and parents to destress," Hannah said.

"She is so good at marketing! Maybe I need to check it out. I'm sure I'll need to destress this fall." Mable said.

"I'm sure Ethan would be happy to help you destress," Hannah said with a wink.

"Dude, really!" Mable said, her face flushing. She flattened her lips, ticked at Hannah.

Ethan laughed. "I'm the manny for two kindergarten boys who love to take things apart and have a loose relationship with following rules. I think I'm going to need to attend that class. Better hand me one of those flyers."

Mable felt her annoyance recede thanks to Ethan's interjection. Once again, he had helped her out, and he didn't even realize that he was making her feel better. She was a goner. How could she not fall for this guy? He instinctively knew what she needed and how to give it to her. "We better get going. We need to get to Kate's so we can drive over for the parade lineup."

"You kids have fun now," Hannah said, and she made the call-me gesture with her hand when Ethan's back was turned to her.

Mable nodded and gave Hannah a thumbs up.

"Hannah is pretty funny," Ethan said.

"She's a riot. Thanks for not taking her seriously."

"Of course, I know how friends can be. Jax is always giving me a hard time. It's how they show they care."

Mable put her hand in Ethan's and gave it a squeeze. They were almost at Kate's store.

Before they could open the door to Pupcakes and Clawssants, Kate burst out of the front door. She had on a cupcake hat that had dog ears.

"Where did you find that hat?" Mable asked.

"Online. I swear, with the right keywords, you can find anything online!"

"It's adorable," Mable said.

"By the way, do you have anything to throw to the kids? Mable says Marley Creek kiddos get pretty cranky if they don't get their free parade candy," Ethan said.

Kate nodded, her hat bobbing. "I'll be right back."

While they waited, Ethan led Iggy over to one of the water bowls Kate had placed outside her store for thirsty pets.

Mable couldn't keep her eyes off Ethan.

The door to the store opened again, and Kate walked out, juggling three large bags. She handed one to Mable and the other to Ethan. Then she locked the door to her store and turned around.

"Check it out," Kate said. She pulled out a couple of pieces of candy from the bag. "They're gummy hot dogs and pet-see-cola bottles!"

"No way," Mable said, and she pulled candy from her bag. "How cute! I've never seen these."

"Guess where I got them?"

"Online," Ethan said.

"Exactly! They are on theme and free of all major allergens," Kate said.

"That's so nice of you, Kate. Most people don't think about allergies when they buy candy to give away; they just think about their favorite candies."

Kate pointed to her shirt. It had a rainbow and the name of her bakery. "Being inclusive is very important to me."

Mable wasn't much of a hugger, or at least she hadn't been much of a hugger, but now she couldn't stop herself from giving Kate a hug, bag of candy and all.

"You guys, thanks again for helping me today!" Kate said.

"Thanks for asking us! It's not very often you get the chance to be in a parade," Ethan said.

"He's right. I've lived here all my life, and this is my first time in the parade," Mable said.

"Well, maybe we'll be able to make this an annual thing. What do you think, Ms. Iggy?" Kate bent down and gave Iggy a pat on the head. When Kate tried to move her hand back, Iggy head-butted her hand, demanding a few more pats.

"Did you see that?" Mable said and looked at Ethan, whose mouth had dropped open.

Ethan nodded. "She didn't try to bite Kate!"

Mable and Ethan did a high five.

"Aww, little Iggy is growing up," Kate said.

Iggy sat on her haunches and started yipping. The three humans laughed, and they walked to the garage where the truck was waiting.

Chapter Twenty-Three

♥

ETHAN

Ethan held out his hand, and Mable boosted herself up and into the truck bed. Kate had placed hay bales in the bed, so they had places to sit during the parade. Kate plopped down on a hay bale. Ethan handed Iggy to Mable, and then he hopped into the truck as well.

Kate closed the tailgate and tapped on the top. "Are you guys good?" She pointed to a small cooler. "I put some waters in there for all of you. Plus, there is a collapsible water bowl for Iggy. Oh, and there is a bag of grain-free treats. They are made with people-safe ingredients, so if you get a hankering for a snack, have at it."

Mable made a face and Ethan just laughed. "I think we're good, Kate, but thanks for letting us know."

"Now I'll have the sliding door open on the cab, so if you need anything, just holler, and thanks again for doing this!" Kate ran around to the driver's door and jumped inside, ready to start the parade.

The truck jerked forward, and Mable was thrown into Ethan. He wrapped his arms around her as if she were the jumbo prize from a carnival game. He breathed in her scent and felt his pulse in his throat. How long would it be until they could be back home so he could worship her?

"Am I squishing you?"

"Not at all. I lo-, I enjoy having you here." He put his hand between her thighs. She leaned into him. He tilted his head and gave her a kiss.

"Mmm, your lips taste like cherries."

"Do you like it? It's a lip gloss. I found it at the bottom of my makeup bag. I forgot I had it."

Ethan licked his lips. "Tastes great."

The wind picked up, and Mable's hair blew toward Ethan. The golden strands brushed against his cheeks, and he could smell a hint of her conditioner. Maybe later they could share a shower. He imagined lathering up his hands and then slowly working his way down her body. His pants tightened.

Mable laughed. She leaned down and whispered in his ear. "You're making me all horny, too."

He pulled her closer to him. They were almost at the parade lineup. "Start thinking about unsexy things. We are about to be in a parade with loads of children present."

She got off his lap and sat next to him. "Dog barf."

"Overflowing trash dumpsters," Ethan said.

"When you accidentally see someone's butt crack."

Ethan shivered. "Okay, I'm ready for the parade."

"Me too." She took her bag of candy and moved over to the other side of the truck.

Main Street was lined on both sides with people three rows deep.

"I don't think we are going to have enough candy!" Mable said.

"Try to only throw it at the kids. Don't let the adults have any!"

"I'll do my best!" Mable said.

She dug into her bag and took out a handful of candy. Ethan watched as she bit her lower lip in concentration. "There!" she said. She launched the candy toward a group of boys wearing baseball uniforms. They scrambled on the ground for the candy like it was a grounder to third base.

Mable waved at the crowd and threw more candy toward a group of moms holding toddlers. The corners of Ethan's mouth turned up. She was having a great time.

"Hey, Mister!" yelled a voice from the crowd on Ethan's side of the street. Ethan turned away from Mable to see who the kid was yelling at. A boy who looked to be about ten was walking alongside the truck. "Hey, Mister!" Ethan's brows lowered. He looked around and didn't see anyone else the kid could be yelling at. He made eye contact with the tow-headed boy and pointed at himself. "Me?"

"Ya, Mister! You got any candy or what?"

"Oh, right," Ethan said. He dug into his bag of candy and tossed a few pieces at the boy.

"Thanks, sir!"

"Polite kid, but I'm too young to be a mister," Ethan mumbled. He grabbed another handful of candy and looked for kids to toss it to.

It wasn't long before their candy supplies were low. Ethan leaned over toward Mable. "We should take turns holding Iggy up so the spectators can see her. That way, we can make the candy last a little longer."

"Great idea. Let me check and see if Kate has any more candy, too," Mable said.

Ethan held Iggy up and waved to the crowd. Iggy barked, and then she licked a paw, and an audible aww could be heard from many in the crowd as they rolled past the group outside Zaina's shop. They were three-quarters of the way through the parade, and Ethan was having a fantastic time. He turned to Mable, who was bending down to talk to Kate through the cab of the truck.

His mouth watered as he watched her taut ass sway from the motion of the truck. She leaned back, pulling the bag of candy out the window, and as she was standing up, Kate had to hit the brakes. Mable fell backwards, and Ethan felt his heart in his throat. He jumped up and caught Mable around the waist. They fell together back onto the hay bales.

"Are you okay?" he asked.

Mable spit out a piece of hay and pushed back her hair. "I'm fine, but look at the candy!"

Candy was all over the bed of the truck, and Iggy was sniffing it. Mable reached over and plucked the hay out of his hair.

"You use the candy we have left, and I'll pick up what fell down," he said.

"Okay, but what about Iggy?"

"I'll watch her."

Mable gave him a thumbs up and tossed candy to the kids on her side and then she switched over to his side. "There's so many kids!" Her face was flushed, and she was grinning.

"You look like you're having the time of your life," he said.

"I'm so glad I could take a break and hang out with you today!" She shouted over the music coming from another float.

"Me too!" He said, his smile wide. He didn't think he'd ever smiled as much as he had over the last week. She made him happier than he could remember being. He quickly picked everything up and added it to their candy bag.

"Just in time," Mable said as she reached in for a handful.

"Good thing we only have a couple of blocks to go."

"Mable!" yelled a chorus of voices.

Mable and Ethan turned to the group yelling her name.

"It's the Jesse's Pub gang. They sure love you," Ethan said.

Mable flipped her hair over her shoulder. "What can I say? I'm loveable."

"You sure are," Ethan said softly.

"Y'all are too old for candy!" Mable yelled back to the group.

"Aw, c'mon!" Lucas the sous chef yelled back.

"Okay, fine!" Mable threw a handful of candy toward her coworkers, and the group scrambled for the gummy candy.

"I haven't seen gummy hot dogs in years," Ethan heard one of them say. He shook his head and turned back to his side of the float. The sun was beating down, and he was glad he'd reminded Mable to wear sunscreen. He took a couple bottles of water out of the cooler and handed one to Mable. She grabbed it and rubbed it over her forehead and then her chest. *Oh, to be that bottle.* And then she cracked it open and took a long drink.

Ethan licked his lips as his mouth was parched. He couldn't wait to get back to Sean and Nicole's. Now that they were past Jesse's Pub, there was only another block and the parade would be over.

Ethan took a big handful of candy and surveyed the crowd, looking to see if there was a bunch of kids he could aim for. A group of adults were sitting in folding chairs, and in front of them were some elementary school-aged kids holding sand buckets of candy. Ethan pulled back his hand to throw when pale skin and jet-black hair highlighted with emerald green caught his eye. It couldn't be her. Distracted, Ethan threw the candy far short of the group.

"Quick, grab the candy before the horses show up!" yelled one of the kids as they scrambled onto the street. Ethan looked over at the children and when he looked back up, he couldn't find the person with hair just like Becca. His eyes must be tired. It couldn't be her. *Could it?*

Chapter Twenty-Four

Mable was distracted as she tried to record her video presentation. This was take twenty-two, and she was ready for a break. Ethan had left this morning to go home and make sure everything was good at the Belmont's, and he'd said he wanted to get some laundry done. Even though she'd told him she was positive Sean and Nicole wouldn't mind if he washed his clothes there, he'd still insisted on leaving.

None of this would have bothered her if not for the fact that after they'd come back yesterday afternoon, Ethan had been quiet. And that wouldn't have been a big deal, but they'd wound up sitting on the couch watching *The Golden Girls,* and he hadn't even kissed her, slid his hand down her thigh, or even tried to cop a feel.

She'd asked him if everything was okay, and he said he was tired. Sure, it had been a long day in the sun, but it wasn't like they were in their forties or something. How tired could he be? No, she knew something else must be going on. She turned off her camera and pushed away from the desk. Her concentration was trashed.

Iggy padded over to her, and Mable decided now was a great time to take her for a walk. They could stop by Zaina's shop and see if Hannah was working. She usually worked on Sundays. As she stood on the front porch, she wondered if she should lock the door and head out, or should she see if Ethan would be back soon and then they could walk Iggy together? She sent him a quick text message.

MABLE: I'm taking a break from the project, going to take Iggy for a walk.

ETHAN: (thumbs up emoji)

Mable paused, trying to decide what to say next. She didn't want to sound needy. She pressed her lips together; she hated how invested she was in Ethan's mood.

MABLE: Do you think you'll be back soon? Should I wait for you?

Mable looked at her phone. The dreaded three dots appeared and disappeared as she stood on the porch, holding Iggy's leash in the other hand. "C'mon," she said out loud, "say you'll be right over."

ETHAN: No, you go on ahead.

"Dammit." Her stomach flip-flopped. She wished she understood what was going on with Ethan. This didn't seem like him. Or was she wrong? Did she only think she knew him? This could be how he acted. How well did she know him, anyway? She stared at her phone, deciding what to say in response.

MABLE: Okay, (dogface emoji)

ETHAN: (thumbs up emoji)

Mable was starting to really hate the thumbs up emoji. She didn't know if it meant sounds good or whatever when he sent it. Until today she would have been sure he meant sounds good! Mable put in her headphones and played one of her favorite mixes. Today, however, her happy playlist wasn't helping. All the good vibes songs were making her think about Ethan. The way Ethan smiled at her, his smell, how he buried his face in her neck when they were cuddling. How he'd buried his face between her legs and given her the best orgasm of her life. She sighed and turned off the music. She'd rather listen to Iggy's nails tapping on the sidewalk as they walked toward New Age Stones and Witch Crafts.

Iggy pulled her along but didn't stop and smell every light post like she had during that first walk with her and Ethan. Mable's stomach roiled.

"What a cute dog!" a young woman exclaimed. Mable pulled up short and drew Iggy's leash to her. "Can I pet her?"

The girl was about her age, with black hair cut in a blunt bob. She had emerald-green highlights and wore dark red lipstick. Her long eyelashes framed her brilliant green eyes. Mable felt like a mess compared to her. Even though she was wearing a pair of flowy capris and a simple cropped tank top, Mable could tell her clothing was high end. This girl must come from money.

The young woman started reaching to pet Iggy with her perfectly manicured hand, and Iggy growled. Mable pulled Iggy back, and she started barking.

"I'm sorry, she's just a puppy. I can't let you pet her. She might nip you."

The girl pouted exaggeratedly and stomped her foot.

Mable repeated, "Sorry," and she shrugged.

"Fine," the girl said tersely and resumed walking.

Mable shook her head and set Iggy down. A minute later, they were greeted by Hannah, who opened the door wide and ushered them into the shop.

"How's my favorite girl doing?" Hannah asked.

"I'm having a kind of down day," Mable said.

Hannah walked toward the tea station. "Actually, I was talking to Iggy."

"Right," Mable smacked her forehead with her hand. "I should have known."

"Sit down in the reading nook. I just finished cleaning up from the tarot reading class and we close soon, so I doubt anyone will be in."

Hannah brought over a small bowl of water for Iggy.

Iggy started lapping up the water.

Hannah pushed her red hair out of her face and looked at her friend. "What can I make for you?"

"Are you trying to make me a potion?"

"You said you were feeling down. It's the perfect time for a potion." The corners of Hannah's mouth turned down in thought. "We have a lemon balm green tea blend called It's Going to be Okay. Can I make you a cup of that?"

"Isn't it too hot for tea?" Mable asked.

"It sounds ridiculous, but drinking hot tea can cool you off."

"That does sound weird, but what the heck. I'll try it."

"Great! Raw sugar, stevia, or honey?" Hannah asked.

"Always honey."

"Do you want to pick your honey? We have five different local honeys."

"You pick."

Hannah hummed as she prepared a cup of the lemon balm tea for both of them. Mable leaned back in the cozy chair and closed her eyes. Just as she was starting to relax, Ethan's face swam up in her mind. She opened her eyes and blinked. Hannah set down her tea on the table in front of Mable, along with a small plate of gingersnaps.

"Since when do you or Zaina bake cookies?"

"Hey, you're the one who doesn't like to bake. I find it relaxing, but these are from Donnie's place."

Mable reached over and nibbled on a cookie, then she took a sip of her tea. "These cookies are delicious."

"I know, right? They go so well with the tea, and ginger is so soothing."

Mable put another couple of cookies on her napkin.

"Do you want to talk about whatever is bothering you now, or do you want to enjoy a tea break while I close the store, and then we'll talk?"

Mable finished her bite of cookie before responding. "The last thing I want is someone in here browsing while I'm sharing my tale of woe, so I'll just wait until you can lock the front door."

"That works!" Hannah got up and walked back over to the counter and began counting down the cash drawer.

Mable was happy to have a little space away from Ethan and her project to relax for a little while. She knew it was time for her to use some of the tools she'd taught students to use this summer. She looked for five things she could see, four things she could feel, three things she could hear, two things she could smell, and one thing she could taste. By the time she was done, Hannah was twisting the lock on the front door.

Hannah sat down across from Mable and much to their surprise, Iggy jumped up into Hannah's lap. "I didn't know she could jump that high!" Mable said.

"You think that's bad; she started jumping onto the bed a few days ago. I hope Sean and Nicole don't mind if she jumps on their bed when they get home."

"Whoops," Hannah said, and she petted Iggy. "Her hair is so silky and she's so sweet now that she's not trying to bite me."

"Speaking of biting, on the way here, this girl came up to me and wanted to pet Iggy. Iggy started growling at her, so I told her no and she got mad about it!"

"Was it a kid?"

"No, she was probably like twenty-one or so. She had super black hair with green highlights. I didn't recognize her. She must be new to Marley Creek or just visiting."

"She's definitely not from around here if you didn't recognize her."

"I can't help it. You know how small towns can be," Mable said.

"Hence why I moved away from mine," Hannah said.

"Exactly, it can be stifling, but for me, I'm always ready to come back after I leave for a week or two."

"I think if Iggy didn't like this person, she probably sucks." Hannah said.

"She tried to bite you the first time you met her," Mable said.

"She is much more mature now and able to tell the difference between an amazing person and one who's not," Hannah said.

Iggy looked at Mable and yipped.

Mable and Hannah burst out laughing.

"See! Just like I told you," Hannah said.

"It was just weird. I don't know why this girl thought she had the right to pet Iggy."

"People are strange."

Mable nodded.

"I know that wasn't why you came here all stressed out. What's going on?"

"It's Ethan. I'm not sure why, but he seems to be distancing himself from me? I don't know."

"Tell me more," Hannah said.

"Friday night we had a great time at Kate's decorating for the pet parade. By the way, she's single, and I'm almost a hundred percent sure she dates women."

Hannah's face turned beet red. "Noted."

"We could go over to her shop together. You could get a few treats for Iggy, or some treats to have here at the shop in case a customer brings their pet. Or wait, I have an idea. Zaina could do a collab with Kate. Pet psychic night!" Mable said.

"That is exactly the kind of offbeat event Zaina would love! I'll have to mention it to her."

"I may not know how to manage my own love life, but I'm going to get you two on a date," Mable said.

"Don't get too distracted here. Let's focus on you."

"Right, back to Friday." Mable looked down, a little embarrassed. "We had sex."

Hannah's mouth dropped. "You did? That's huge! How was it? Wait, if it was great, you would have told me by now."

"It was...good."

Hannah squinted at Mable. "So, not great?"

"It was a little uncomfortable. I didn't hate it and I'd really like to give it another go." Mable felt heat break out across her chest. This conversation was so awkward she could hardly believe she was having it.

"Did you tell him how you feel? Is that when he started acting standoffish?"

"I wanted to try doing it again Saturday night and see if we could make it better for me, and we had a great time at the parade, so I was sure it was going to happen, but after that he was quiet."

"At least we know that he isn't the kind of guy who'd get his panties in a bunch because you wanted to talk about how to make sex more enjoyable for you."

"He's so good at giving me what I need, and he asked me at, ah, various points if I was enjoying what he was doing when we were, ah, doing other stuff." Mable fanned herself. "I can't believe this conversation."

"It's okay to have frank conversations about sex stuff," Hannah said.

"I know. It's just my mom never talked about sex stuff except to tell me not to have any because it ruins a woman's life," Mable said.

"She's pretty bitter for someone who had five kids after you and is still married to the guy she met in college."

"She's a puzzle, that's for sure," Mable said, "and so it seems is Ethan. Last night we watched TV, and he wasn't interested in even holding my hand. It was a long day, and it was crazy hot during the parade, so maybe he was just tired."

"That makes sense."

"Except today he went back home to do laundry he could have simply done at the house," Mable said.

"Could you be overthinking it?"

"I have a bad feeling, but I don't know why. What should I do?" Mable asked.

"Let me think." Hannah leaned back in the chair and crossed her legs. Iggy jumped down and made her way over to Mable. She flopped down on the floor and put her head on her paws. "I guess, text him and see if he plans to be by you for dinner, and if he does, then ask him if something is wrong."

"And hopefully he will tell me."

"All you can do is ask, right?" Hannah said.

Mable bit her lip. "Yep." She got up and snapped the leash back onto Iggy.

Hannah stood up, and they walked to the front door. Hannah unlocked the door. Mable turned and gave Hannah a hug. "I don't know what I'd do without you."

"If you need anything, call me, but Ethan's a good guy. I'm sure everything is going to be fine," Hannah said.

Chapter
Twenty-Five

♥

Ethan watched his clothes tumble in the front-loading dryer. It was happening again. Ever since he'd seen that woman in the crowd who looked like Becca, he'd been spiraling. Was it her? Why would she be in Marley Creek, and if it was her, why should he care? He pulled out his phone. He should call his therapist. It was Sunday though, and he didn't want to go as far as saying he needed emergency help.

"You can help yourself." He said out loud, then mumbled, "choose your focus." For a moment, Mable's face supplanted Becca's in his mind. He'd given her the brush-off today, and that was dumb. He pulled out his phone to text Mable and a text popped up from a number he didn't recognize.

248-555-1212: Ethan, It's Becca. I'm in Marley Creek. We've got to talk.

Ethan stared at the phone and re-read the message as a humming sound began building in his ears. He felt flushed, and on the third re-read, sweat was beading on his forehead.

It had been her! She was here in his town. What was she doing here, and why did she need to talk to him? His finger hovered. After everything that had happened, he should just block her number. He didn't owe her anything.

He put down his phone and paced the laundry room. The scent of freshly washed clothes was one of his favorite calming scents, but it sure wasn't helping him now. His stomach roiled, and saliva built up in his mouth. His throat started to close, and he rushed to the bathroom. He put up the lid and kneeled in front of the toilet. Within seconds, he'd thrown up his lunch.

Becca's timing was shit. Just when he'd finally, finally been able to open up to the idea of dating again, here she came. He couldn't not reply. If he blocked her, he would always wonder why she'd come to Marley Creek. He opened a drawer, got his toothbrush, and brushed his teeth. Once he was done, he walked back to his bedroom. He sat down on the floor and thought about his reply.

ETHAN: I thought I saw you at the pet parade.

248-555-1212: Yes! That was me! Are you free tonight?

Ethan dropped his phone on the carpet and put his head in his hands. He didn't want to be free tonight. He wanted to be hanging out with Mable, but even as he thought about sitting on the couch with Mable, his arm wrapped around her, smelling her floral scent, Becca's green eyes and her pouty lips creeped into his mind.

Was he truly over her? Suddenly he wasn't sure and there was only one road to that answer, and that road went through Becca. The question now was what to say to Mable. They'd never had a relationship talk, sure, they'd been cohabitating and parenting a dog for the week, but what exactly were they to each other?

He texted Becca first. As he started typing his response, a text from Mable popped up on his phone.

MABLE: Hey Ethan, just checking to see if you wanted to get carry-out from Jesse's tonight?

He read her text, and his chest tightened. Ethan felt pulled in two directions. He pushed her text aside and went back to messaging Becca.

Ethan: I'm not free tonight. I can meet you tomorrow night at Hop's Heaven.

Ethan figured if he met Becca at Hop's Heaven, he'd have Jax there for support, and better yet, he could go early and talk this mess over with them. Before he could switch over to reply to Mable, Becca answered him.

BECCA: That will work. How about seven p.m.?

Ethan hit a quick thumbs-up emoji and switched back to Mable's text.

ETHAN: I'd love to get carryout from Jesse's. Do you think they would give us a mini burger for Iggy?

MABLE: I'll ask! What time should I order?

Ethan checked the time.

ETHAN: Give me twenty minutes and then order. I'll pick it up on the way to Sean and Nicole's.

MABLE: (burger emoji plus dog face emoji plus laughing emoji)

Ethan replied with a laughing emoji and put his phone in his pocket. His nerves were jangling. His heart was beating in his throat. The right thing to do was tell Mable that Becca was in town and he was meeting her tomorrow. Beyond tomorrow, he did not know what was going to happen. If Becca had come to Marley Creek two weeks ago, it would have been so clear cut. But now he wasn't sure he knew what he wanted.

He finished his laundry and instead of taking some of the clean clothes with him; he left everything at home. He needed to sort out some things before he spent the night with Mable again; doing anything else didn't feel right. Ethan made sure the house was locked and the alarm was on, and he got into the minivan to pick up their food from Jesse's Pub.

When he was in Jesse's Pub waiting for someone to get his order from the back, he sent a quick text to Jax.

ETHAN: You working tomorrow night?

Jax responded as Ethan gave a tip to the server who handed him his food. When he got into the car, he read the text.

JAX: I'm closing, what's up?

> ETHAN: Long story short, Becca is in town and wants to talk. I said I'd meet her tomorrow at Hop's Heaven.

> JAX: Dude.

> ETHAN: I know. I'll be there about six. Think you'll have time to talk?

> JAX: I'll make time.

> ETHAN: Thanks, I'll see you then.

Ethan started the car and drove toward Sean and Nicole's. As he got closer, anxiety caused his muscles to tighten. He tried to relax his jaw, but it was no use. His stomach was souring. He wasn't sure what he was going to say to Mable. Why did things have to get so complicated?

A weight was on his chest again. He remembered that weight had been a constant companion during the last few months he'd been with Becca. He should have known she was going to leave him before she did.

There had also been amazing times, like when he'd gone home with her for winter break after they'd first started dating. Her family had treated him like one of their own, and by the time the break was over, Ethan had been added to the family chat. What a Christmas morning that was! Becca and her three brothers, plus their wives and kids. Becca's dad had dressed as Santa, and her mom had made a gourmet spread for breakfast. He'd felt like he was in a Hallmark Christmas movie. Ethan couldn't help but smile at that memory.

He knocked on the door and waited for Mable to answer. He shifted his weight from foot to foot as he waited. Sweat was breaking out under his arms.

Mable opened the door, and he was stunned again by her simple beauty. Her long hair was in a messy top knot. She was wearing an Illinois State tank top and a pair of cutoffs. All he wanted to do was pick her up and drag her off to the bedroom and show her how gorgeous he found every part of her.

"Outstanding, you're here. Come on in."

She held the door open, and he walked through, breathing in her scent as he passed her. His cock rose to attention. *God, she smelled good.*

Iggy barked and ran around him demanding his attention, so he put the bag of carry-out on the counter. He kicked off his shoes, picked up Iggy, and gave her some cuddles.

"How'd it go with the laundry?" she asked.

He knew she was trying to keep things light. She had to be confused about his behavior last night and earlier today. Things were only going to get worse. He tried to talk himself into not mentioning anything about Becca tonight. Maybe he should wait, meet up with Becca, and see why she was in town before he said anything to Mable. For all he knew, maybe Becca wanted to talk to him about something that had nothing to do with their previous relationship. His breathing quickened as he wrestled with what to say to Mable. "I know this sounds weird, but I find the smell of laundry soap relaxing."

"I don't think it's that strange. You can't be the only one. There are laundry-scented candles out there," Mable said.

"Candles that smell like laundry soap? For real?" Ethan said.

"I can't believe you've never heard of that. I'll have to see if there are any at Zaina's shop for sale. I'll buy you one."

Ethan instantly sobered. He had made plans to meet his ex tomorrow evening, and Mable was about to buy him something he might like. He had to tell her about Becca tonight.

"I got some of that seltzer water you like earlier today. Did you want a glass with ice for it?" She asked.

Ethan's heart squeezed. This was agony, and he didn't know when it was the best time to tell Mable. He dropped his shoulders. There would not be a good time. He set Iggy down went to the counter and unpacked the food while Mable got their drinks.

Once they had their plates of food; they sat down at the table. Ethan took a bite of his dinner, and it could have been a pile of sawdust for all he tasted. His throat felt as if it were going to close. He was going to miss this. It was so easy to be with Mable.

"How was your day? Did you get a lot done on your project?"

Mable dropped her eyes to the table. "I was struggling earlier. I couldn't stay focused, so I wound up taking a break and walking over to see Hannah."

"And did that help?"

Mable looked into his eyes. "I'm feeling much better now."

Ethan gulped, "That's good." And then he started shoveling the rest of his dinner into his mouth.

Iggy was under the table, and she was trying to lick his feet. He kept moving his feet, and as soon as he did, she was back at it.

"What's going on?" Mable said, giving him a confused look.

"Iggy keeps trying to lick my feet."

Mable laughed and the sound of it was like a dagger to his heart. He was already missing their time together. He reached over and cupped her cheek.

"I love your laugh."

"Really? It always seems so loud to me," Mable said.

"No, it's not too loud, and even if it were, I'd still love it."

He watched as a blush rose up her chest. He moved his hand back and took a drink of his seltzer water.

"Did you need to put on some socks or something?" she asked.

"It's okay, I'll be fine. She's probably hoping I'll drop food so she can snag it."

They went back to eating and after a little while, Iggy gave up and left the dining area. It was so quiet that they could hear when Iggy found a squeaky toy in the living room and started growling at it.

"Um, so, after dinner, did you want to watch a movie or," she paused, "do something else?"

Ethan's chest felt heavy. His throat was trying to close again. "Actually, I probably need to go home."

"Oh," Mable said.

He put his napkin and silverware on his plate and picked it up. "Can I take your plate?"

"Sure, I don't think I want to eat anymore." Her voice was quiet and monotone.

It made his heart ache. He picked up her plate and avoided her eyes. Once the garbage was in the trash, he scraped their plates and put them in the dishwasher along with the silverware. Then he sat back down and moved his chair next to her.

"Can I hold your hand?"

"Okay," Mable said.

He took her hand in his. It was moist with perspiration, and he was sure his was clammy too.

She took a shaky breath. He did too.

"Yesterday, I thought I saw Becca at the end of the parade, and it really threw me off."

Mable brightened a little. "It's okay," she said.

He continued, "Then this afternoon, I got a text from a number I didn't recognize."

Mable froze.

"It was Becca. She's in Marley Creek and she wants to talk." Ethan stared down at their hands, still intertwined.

Mable sniffed quietly.

"I don't know what she wants to talk about, but I agreed to meet with her tomorrow night."

Mable let go of his hand and got up to get a paper towel. She used it to dab her eyes. Ethan felt sick. He took a few gulping breaths, trying to keep his dinner down. He forced himself to look Mable in the eyes. If he was going to hurt her, he should have to see her pain.

"Mable, I'm so sorry, but I've got to talk to her and find out what's going on."

"What if she wants to get back together? Is that what you want?" she asked.

"A couple of months ago, I would have said yes, without a doubt," Ethan said.

"And now?"

"I don't know. Mable, I care about you," he said.

Mable laughed bitterly.

"I do. I care about you a lot."

Mable clicked her tongue and wiped her eyes. Her lips turned down.

"Becca and I were together for two years. I called her parents Mom and Dad. I need to talk to her. I owe her that."

"Where was she when you couldn't function? You didn't seem to owe her then."

Ethan sighed. Part of him was happy that Mable cared enough about him to point out Becca's mistreatment of him, and the rest of him felt terrible for breaking her heart and his.

She sat back down at the table, and he reached over to push her hair behind her ear.

"Don't," she said, and he put his hand back down. "Please don't touch me now."

"I'm sorry," he whispered.

"You should go," she said.

He pushed his chair back from the table, and Iggy barked and left her squeaky toy behind to see what was happening with them.

"If you need any help with Iggy, just text me."

"We'll be fine," she said, and raised her chin.

"I left some stuff in the bedroom."

She waved her hand. "Better go get it then."

He walked back into the bedroom and picked up his toiletry bag off the dresser and a pair of socks he'd forgotten to grab earlier off the floor. Mable was still sitting at the table. Her arms crossed.

"Mable," he said.

"What?" she said and blew out a sigh.

"I'm so sorry."

"Right now, I find that hard to believe. If you were sorry, if you cared about me, I don't think you'd be doing this."

Ethan put on his shoes by the door. He put his hand on the doorknob and then turned back to Mable. "I—" he stopped talking. He didn't know what to say that could make either of them feel better. It was probably better if he just stopped talking and let her be.

"Bye, Ethan," she said with a finality that broke his heart.

Iggy trotted over to the door and pawed at his leg. He gave her one last pat. Then he opened the door and walked out.

Chapter Twenty-Six

♥

Mable sat in front of her computer. The camera was on, and she knew she looked like shit. Her eyes were bloodshot and puffy from spending the night crying. Her face was pale, and she was so jittery she couldn't type a sentence without major typos. She was a wreck and had only herself to blame.

If she had stayed focused on her project and not allowed herself to fall for Ethan, she'd probably have this project complete and she wouldn't be so sad. She could barely stand to be in this room. All it did was remind her of their time together and how she'd let him in. For years she'd avoided love and sex because it was a distraction that could derail her dreams, and now here she was, a broken-hearted mess with a project due.

Iggy ran into the room and barked at Mable. She knew by now that this bark was Iggy's 'I've got to go to the potty' bark. "Saved by the puppy," she said and walked to the backdoor as Iggy raced ahead. Mable sat on the chaise lounge and watched Iggy sniffing around the yard before doing her business. Once she was done, Mable didn't call her up to the deck. Given a choice between sitting outside listening to the cicadas scream and being inside staring at her computer screen, she'd take the fresh air for now. Mable's phone vibrated in her back pocket. She rushed to pull it out of her pocket and it clattered to the ground, bouncing off the two steps down from the deck onto the stone path.

"Oh, no!" she shouted, and she ran to pick up her phone. The fuss she was making had Iggy running to her side. She picked up the phone and turned it over. *Just my luck, the screen is broken.* The phone was still working, but she was going to need to get it fixed as soon as possible. A voicemail notification popped up on the screen. She couldn't see who'd left her a voicemail. She clicked play, her whole-body tensing as she hoped it was Ethan.

Something must have happened to her speaker because the voice sounded tiny and far away. It was definitely female, however. She put the phone to her ear and pressed play again.

Iggy was in the yard chasing a moth.

"Hi Mable, it's Susan. I wanted to do a quick check-in, see if you'd like a set of eyes on your project before you turn it in. I've got some free time on my hands this week. Just let me know."

The corners of Mable's lips turned up. How lucky she was to have a mentor who cared as much as Susan did. She decided if she didn't have her shit together by tomorrow, she'd call Susan and ask for help. She put her phone into her back pocket and then she thought better of it. Maybe she could find some clear packing tape and use that to fix her screen so she could touch the screen without getting her finger cut.

Iggy was sniffing around the yard, so Mable stretched out on the chaise lounge and tried to relax, but everything about being at Sean and Nicole's was marked by her time with Ethan. Even sitting here reminded her of when he was lying on this lounger. His tank top had stuck to him with sweat, and she'd first noticed his washboard abs. Heat built between her thighs, and that just ticked her off. How dare the thought of him get her libido running wild. "You need to snap out of it, Weaverton," she said to the backyard.

She made a deal with herself. She'd work on her project, not just stare at the screen for two more hours, and then she could call Hannah and wallow about Ethan for the rest of the night. Provided Hannah was willing to deal with her weepy self. "Time to go inside, Iggy!"

Iggy was pawing at the gate in the far back of the yard.

"Iggy! Treat time!"

Iggy stopped digging and looked up. Then she turned and trotted back to Mable.

"Good girl!"

Iggy ran past Mable and started pawing at the back door.

"Simmer down, Missy." Mable opened the door, and Iggy ran over to her dog bowl and sat down.

"You are such a smart puppy!" Mable took out the jar of puppy treats and held one in her hand.

"Stay."

Iggy's tongue had been sticking out, and she put it back in her mouth.

Mable held out the treat. Iggy delicately put her teeth on the end of it and pulled it off Mable's hand, and then she ran into the living room.

Mable rubbed her chest with her hand. Ethan would have been so impressed with Iggy's self-control. She swallowed back a ragged sigh and started walking down the hall. When she got to the main bedroom, she poked her head in and took a big intake of breath. Then she let it out. This room didn't smell like Ethan!

Mable gathered up all her project materials and brought them into the main bedroom. She could work at Nicole's vanity, still have a door to shut so she could tape without street noise, and most importantly, be in an Ethan-free space.

Her timer went off. She saved her video edits and closed the laptop. When she'd made her schedule for this project, she didn't have any experience editing video, and now she realized it was going to take hours longer than she'd budgeted for. She bit her lip and pulled back her hair, braiding it into a quick side braid. Then she shook it out and re-braided it. She was so close to finishing this project. Now she was regretting the time she'd spent with Ethan. If she'd known then what she knew now! She frowned. This "if only" talk was the worst thing to do, and she knew that logically, but it was so hard to stop. Mable hoped talking with Hannah would be cathartic and help her focus. She only had six days left.

Mable tapped on her phone. She'd found packing tape and put it over the broken screen, and it seemed to help. She texted Hannah.

MABLE: Please tell me you aren't busy.

HANNAH: I'm not busy.

MABLE: Seriously tho, are you busy?

HANNAH: I'm at the gym, what's up?

MABLE: Can you come over after the gym?

HANNAH: You still at Sean and Nicole's?

MABLE: Yep, and can you bring a bottle of margaritas?

HANNAH: Ethan problems?

MABLE: You could say that. Just get here soon.

HANNAH: (heart-hands emoji)

MABLE: (gif of someone saying I love you)

Mable glimpsed herself in the hallway mirror. Her shirt had ketchup on it, and her face could only be described as greasy. She got a towel out of the hall closet and went to take a shower. The cascading water helped to wash away a little of the sadness hanging on her. She took her time washing, exfoliating, and then finally moisturizing her skin. She threw on a pair of soft shorts and a cropped T-shirt and left the bathroom.

Her phone vibrated on the kitchen counter. Her heart lurched. She lunged for her phone, and this time she didn't drop it.

"Hello."

"I'm here. I texted you a couple of times, but you didn't answer," Hannah said.

"Sorry, I was taking a shower. I'm walking over to the door now."

"Kay."

Mable opened the door and Hannah burst in.

"The mosquitoes were trying to suck me dry out there. Where do you want this?" She had a bottle of premixed classic margaritas in one hand and a bag of tortilla chips in the other. "I hope you have salsa."

"I do, but I only have mild." Mable said.

Hannah frowned. "It'll have to do." Then she brightened. "Mind if I look for hot sauce in the fridge?"

"Be my guest."

Hannah toed off her shoes and put her stuff on the table.

Mable pulled out a couple of mason jars. "Do you want me to get out the blender and make slushy margaritas, or are you good with on the rocks?"

Hannah was rummaging through the condiments in the refrigerator door. "It's your party; whatever works for you."

"On the rocks, then." Mable put a few ice cubes in each of their jars and then poured her drink right to the top. She picked it up and took a sip. "Oh, that's good." She took a long drink and walked over to the table, carrying each of their glasses along.

"Ooo," Hannah said, "this looks good. Jalapeno lime hot sauce."

"Go for it," Mable said.

Hannah brought the hot sauce over to the table.

Mable took a handful of chips and put them on her plate, along with a couple of spoonfuls of salsa. Hannah did the same and then shook hot sauce on top of her salsa.

Mable held up her glass. "To an amazing woman who skips leg day for her friends."

Hannah clinked her glass against Mable's and they each took a drink. "Joke's on you. I skipped my core workout."

"My toast still stands."

They each loaded a chip with salsa and crunched.

Hannah took a drink of her margarita and waited until Mable's mouth wasn't full to ask, "So, what did he do?"

"Remember how I thought something was off the other day?"

Hannah nodded.

"He thought he saw his ex at the pet parade."

"Okay?"

"Yesterday she texted him, said she was in town and wanted to talk to him," Mable said.

"Wow."

"I know. So, I guess he's going to get back together with her."

"Did he say that?" Hannah asked.

"No, but he's going to meet up with her. What else could happen?"

"Didn't she treat him like crap?"

"They were living together, and one day he came home and she was just gone." Mable said.

"Who does that?"

"I guess she couldn't deal with breaking up with him face-to-face, so she moved out and sent him a text."

"She full on moved out and then sent a breakup text, and now he's meeting with her to talk. Were you the first person he's dated since her?"

"I'm not a hundred percent sure, but yes, I think so."

"It's like her wicked spidey senses started tingling and she knew he was over her."

"Well, I don't know if he's over her."

"Come on Mable, of course he is. If he wasn't, do you think y'all would have had sex? Does he seem like that kind of guy?"

Mable was getting teary again. She wiped her eyes with the back of her hand, and then she got up and got a tissue. She sat back down. "Ready for a refill?"

"Only half a glass. I've got to drive home," Hannah said.

"You could stay here," Mable said quickly.

Hannah reached over and patted her arm. "Honey, do you need me to stay?"

"Please," Mable said.

"Then I'll stay." Hannah raised her glass. "Fill'er up."

Mable topped off their glasses and sat back down, relieved. "I could really use girl time tonight."

"I'll make sure you don't accidentally text Ethan." Hannah said.

"Thank you."

Hannah got up and wrapped Mable in a hug.

"You give the best hugs, Hannah, and you always smell like lavender."

"It's my favorite essential oil. I have a roll on." Hannah released her and sat back down, taking a long drink.

"You're right," Mable finally said.

"About what?" Hannah said.

"Ethan must have been over her."

"Exactly," Hannah said, "and now that I know more about his ex, I'm not thrilled he is meeting her."

"Same. I'm so not thrilled," Mable said.

"He should have told her anything she had to say to him could clearly be done via text and left it at that," Hannah said.

"Yes! Now I'm getting more mad than sad!"

"I hope we are doing the stages of grief right," Hannah said.

"Ugh, I don't want to be sad or mad. I just want Ethan back."

"Look, I don't want to get your hopes up, but I don't think Ethan will get back with his ex, even if she came all the way here to talk to him."

"You really think so?"

Hannah crunched up one of the ice cubes in her empty glass. "Oh my God, I just had a thought. When did they break up?"

"Um, in the fall, I'm not sure when, why?" Mable said.

"What if she were pregnant, and he's the dad?"

"I hope that's the booze talking," Mable said. Her heart started pounding. Could Ethan be a dad? "If I've fallen for a guy that knocked up someone in college and now she's coming to tell him and then he is going to feel obligated to marry her, I will lose my shit. Give me my phone. I've got to text him."

Hannah put Mable's phone down her shirt. "I will not let you call him! You'll regret it."

Mable poured the rest of the bottle into their glasses.

"I know it seems dark right now and I know your heart is breaking, but I don't think your story with Ethan is over."

"I want to believe you're right, but I'm afraid to hope. I feel like I'm better off if I give up and try not to think about him and make myself focus on school," Mable said.

"I stand by my vibes. The vibes say he really likes you. Now that being said, I'm here for you. If you want to assume that he's going back to his ex and you need to get over him, I'll support you in that, too."

"You're making me get all choked up again. You're the best," Mable said.

"I love you too," Hannah said.

Mable yawned widely. "I don't want to think about Ethan anymore today. It just makes me sad or hopefully sad. Hopefully sad makes me want to wrestle you to the ground so I can get my phone and text him.

"I mean, do your worst. I think I can take you," Hannah said."

Mable finished her drink and set her glass down hard on the table. "I think I've been over-served."

"Let me guess, the tortilla chips were your dinner." Hannah said.

"Bingo."

"Honey, that's not good. Let me go get you some water." Hannah stood up, found the cabinet where the cups were stored, and got Mable some water.

"Thanks for the water. I need it."

Hannah patted Mable on the shoulder. "How about if we order a pizza and watch *The Golden Girls*?"

"That would be amazing."

Hannah fished Mable's phone out of her bra and ordered pizza.

Chapter Twenty-Seven

♥

Ethan sat at the bar, nursing a Marley Creek Marzen lager, waiting for Jax to close out a customer tab so they could talk. He tapped anxiously on the bar and looked at his reflection in the large mirror behind the bar. He ran a hand through his hair and then smoothed it out. The mirror had proven to be very useful in his wait to meet Becca. Now that it was less than an hour until she was supposed to be here, he couldn't tear his eyes away. He'd never simultaneously wanted to see and not see someone in his life.

"Dude," Jax said, giving Ethan a glass of water. "You look like shit."

Ethan looked around Jax and into the mirror again. "You think?" He straightened his red polo shirt.

"You have major bags under your eyes, and you look like you are waiting for a job interview to start. Please tell me you're not wearing khaki pants."

Ethan scoffed, "Not pants, of course not. It's like ninety degrees outside; I'm wearing cargo shorts."

"What time is your annual job review at Target?"

"Bro, what are you?" then it clicked for Ethan. "Oh, I get it. You're saying I look like I work at Target."

"Exactly," Jax said. "That sure took you a while."

"I can't think straight, and Becca is supposed to be here in," he looked at his phone. "Twenty-eight minutes."

"What if she doesn't show?"

"Oh, she'll show. The only reason for her to be in Marley Creek is me. It's not like she has family or friends here. She lives in Livonia, Michigan."

"Michigan? Damn, she did come quite a way just to see you."

"I'm freaking out," Ethan said.

"She really gets to you, huh?"

"You know about what all happened between us."

Jax nodded. "If you ask me—"

"I am one hundred percent asking you for any and all advice you can give me."

"Right, so I think she's a real piece of work and you should tell her to pound sand." Jax said.

"Pound sand?"

"I picked that up from some of the plumbers who come in. I guess it's a polite way to say fuck off."

"Oh, I got that," Ethan said.

Jax nodded to someone standing at the end of the bar. "I'll be right back."

Ethan took a drink of water and checked his phone to see if Becca had texted him. Then he looked down at his outfit. He did look as if he worked in retail. What had he been thinking?

Not that it mattered. If what he was wearing made Becca turn around and leave, it wouldn't break him like it had before.

Jax returned to the spot by Ethan. "Do you want another beer?"

"I'll just wait until Becca shows up to have one," he said.

"That's probably a good idea. So why are you meeting her, anyway? You seemed like you were having a great time hanging out with Mable."

Ethan blew out a breath, and the corners of his lips turned down. "How can I not meet her, though? I was planning to ask her to marry me."

Jax rubbed their tattooed arm sleeve. "Sometimes plans change." Jax tapped on the bar with their knuckles and said, "Are you going to choose your future or your past?" Then they walked away to fill the growler of a regular who was at the pickup window.

Ethan looked down at the bar, the words Jax said echoing in his head. A hand tapped him on the shoulder, and he jumped.

A giggle he hadn't heard in a long time sounded behind him. Ethan's heart was racing now. He breathed in, and the scent of caramel and brown sugar made his stomach roil. "Becca, it's really you." He said as he took her in.

Becca put her arms out. She was so much tinier than Mable. He'd forgotten she was barely five feet tall. She was wearing a sequined black halter top and a super-short skirt. He could see the birthmark she had on her mid-thigh. How many times had he traced that birthmark with his hand, with his tongue?

"Is there somewhere we can go to talk?" she asked.

"You don't want to sit here?" He tapped the chair next to him.

Becca scrunched up her face. "At the bar? No, thank you."

Ethan shrugged. "Okay, let me see." He looked around the taproom and saw a booth at the far end of the room, right by the bathrooms. It would have to do. "We can sit over there," he said, pointing.

"Okay," Becca said, and she put her hand in his.

Her familiar soft hand was back in his, and he couldn't stop himself from comparing it to Mable's hand. Becca had short, blunt fingers he knew she hated, and so she always had expensive acrylic nails because she wanted to elongate her fingers. Mable had short nails because she said it was easier to type. He didn't think he'd even seen Mable wearing nail polish. He led the way over to the table, and once they were there, he sat down.

"Can I sit next to you?" Becca asked, batting her fake eyelashes.

"Ah, sure." Ethan slid down to make room for Becca next to him. His chest tightened. He felt trapped. She cozied up to him and again that brown sugar and caramel scent wafted over him, making his stomach churn. He moved away from Becca as politely as possible.

"Thanks for meeting with me," she said.

Ethan kept quiet. The less he talked, the sooner he'd know why she'd come to Marley Creek.

"Pookie, I've missed you so much. I don't think you realize how hard it has been for me." She pouted and then she licked her lips and put her hand on his thigh.

He was glad his shorts were on the longer side. He didn't want her touching his skin. His brows furrowed. He'd wanted her so badly just a few months ago, and even a couple of weeks ago he would have been elated to be in her presence, but now he wished he was hanging out at Sean and Nicole's with Mable.

"What's been going on, Becca?"

She fluttered her eyelashes. "Well, you would not believe how many times this summer everyone has been asking about you! Mom and Dad can't stop talking about last summer at the cabin. 'Remember when Ethan organized craft night?' 'Oh Becca, do you know how Ethan made that yummy summer cocktail we had last summer?' 'How is Ethan?' 'What do you mean you haven't talked to him in months?'" She threw her hands up in the air. "It was so annoying, like hello people, I'm right here, why can't we focus on Becca, why is everyone missing Ethan?"

Ethan frowned. "Poor Becca," he said, and his thoughts wandered. He wondered how Iggy was doing. He should have bought more treats from Kate the other day, so Mable would have them on hand in case Iggy started acting up because he wasn't there.

"So, then I said..."

Ethan realized he'd zoned out and wasn't even sure what Becca was talking about. He looked over at Jax behind the bar. His past or his future. Boy, Jax had really nailed it. He didn't even know why he was still here. He could be with Mable right now.

"Pookie, can you believe she said that?"

He knew that cue. "No, Becca, I cannot."

"I knew you'd be on my side. So how soon can you pack up? If we leave in an hour, we can be at the cabin before midnight."

Ethan's mouth dropped open. "I'm sorry, what?"

"Weren't you listening? I need you to come with me up to the cabin 'til Labor Day. I can't take another second of these people asking about you. Once you're there, they'll remember all your flaws and stop acting like you are some perfect guy."

"This is a strange way to ask me to get back together with you."

Becca shook her head. "Oh, Pookie, I don't want to start dating again. I just want you to come up to the cabin and help me get my family off my back. I drove all the way down here. The least you can do is help me out. Besides, I know you love the cabin and my family paying for everything."

Ethan stood straight. "What are you insinuating?"

"Come on, be real. Before I came along, all you had was your scholarship, your Walmart wardrobe, and a park district gym body." She squeezed his leg. "Speaking of that body, let's get out of here and back to my hotel room."

Ethan moved Becca's hand off his thigh and turned toward her so that he could be sure she was looking at him. "Unlike you, I never judged you or treated you differently based on your family's money. Did I ever ask them to pay for anything? Did I ever expect them to give me anything? Did I expect to be invited along on any of your family trips?"

Becca crossed her arms. "I don't like how you are acting. Be real right now. Let's go get a bag packed for you and get on the road."

"I'm not going anywhere, and I most definitely am not going to have sex with you. I don't know why you thought you could drive all the way here, and I'd drop everything to be a prop for you."

Becca scrunched up her face. "Are you joking right now? I thought you were dying to spend time with me. I mean, you dropped out of college after we broke up. Everyone said you were devastated."

Ethan shook his head, thinking about all those days when he had been laid low by Becca. Those days were so over. God, this meeting was a mistake. He should have taken Jax and Mable's advice and blocked Becca's number. But here he was, and she was so, so much his past.

"Let me be super clear. We are over. We aren't friends. We aren't fuck buddies. Lose my number."

Becca slid out of the booth. "You're making a big mistake, Ethan."

"Am I, though?" Ethan said and flashed a smile.

Becca stomped her foot. "Fuck off, Ethan."

"More like pound sand, Becca."

Becca frowned. "What?"

Ethan chuckled. "Nothing, absolutely nothing."

"This is your last chance, Ethan."

Ethan folded his hands. "I'm good."

"Fine, then." Becca spun on her heel and flounced out.

Ethan grinned from ear-to-ear. He should be mad about the things Becca said, but right now, he felt like he could run a four-minute mile.

He got out of the booth and went up to the bar.

"Jax, can I get another beer now?"

"Sure thing." Jax poured Ethan a beer and placed it in front of him. "So, what happened?"

"I don't know if I could even explain what just happened."

"Try," Jax said.

Chapter Twenty-Eight

♥

Hannah had left first thing in the morning, right as rain, but Mable was nursing a pounding headache. This was why she didn't drink much. The margaritas were too tasty, and she was too much of a lightweight to handle the alcohol hidden in the sweet taste. Mable took a couple of acetaminophen and then fed Iggy her breakfast. She picked up her phone and put it on the charger. Hannah had hidden it under a couch cushion last night, leaving the battery to die.

She had three new text messages:

HANNAH: Want me to do a tarot card reading? See if Ethan is your destiny?

SUSAN MENTOR: Checking in, how is the project?

BOSS MAN: (image) please show this to Iggy.

Mable clicked on the image showing Sean and Mable wearing Scottish tartan garb and holding a tiny matching outfit for Iggy.

Mable called Iggy over to her. Iggy jumped into her lap. She showed Iggy the phone. "Look, Iggy, it's your silly mom and dad. They are going to be back in just a few more days."

Then she texted back to Sean.

MABLE: Iggy misses her Mommy and Daddy. She can't wait for you to get home so she can show you all the cool tricks she's learned.

"Now Iggy, you know the time difference is big, so they won't see your reply for a while." Mable looked back on the last week and a half with Iggy, and her heart swelled with pride. The first day had been a total disaster, but now she was confident in her ability to know what Iggy needed and to give it to her.

An idea bubbled up from her subconscious. What if, instead of trying to work around Iggy for her video presentation, maybe she could put Iggy in it? She ran to the bedroom to rework her script. Until now, she had felt like her presentation lacked a throughline and because of that, it was too scattered. Which made sense, she'd been feeling scattered as she worked on it. First, because she hadn't known how to take care of a puppy, then second, the push-pull of Ethan. She forced Ethan out of her head for now.

Mable texted Susan back and discussed her idea to add Iggy to the video portion of her project and Susan was completely on board.

SUSAN MENTOR: Would you like to send me your video presentation once it is done? I'm finished packing for my move home and have time to review it.

MABLE: That would be amazing. If all goes well, I will have it ready for your feedback on Friday.

SUSAN MENTOR: I'll look for your email.

MABLE: Thanks again!

Mable looked back at the text from Hannah. She was just going to leave that one alone. Right now, her headache had receded, and she had a project to finish. She'd let herself think about him later. Mable set a timer and got to work. She grabbed a red pen and began changing her script.

A few hours later, Mable's stomach was growling. She saved her work and walked into the kitchen to see if there was anything she could munch on. She opened the refrigerator and stared into it. The only things in the fridge were a few sad-looking pieces of celery and a single snack pack of hummus.

Iggy was running around the house with a case of the zoomies. Now was a good time for both of them to get fresh air. Mable put on her crossbody bag and clipped on Iggy's leash. She wanted to get something quick, and she also wanted to get snacks for Iggy, so she decided to walk over to Kate's shop for Iggy and then get a slice of pizza and a cola from Best Pizza Near Me. The moment the leash was on Iggy, she was pulling Mable to the door.

"Iggy, you need to be patient and follow me. Remember, I'm the leader of the pack." Mable's heart ached. The pack was missing Ethan. She wondered if he was out on a date with his ex. Hannah had been so sure that Ethan wasn't going to get back together with Becca. But here it was, the day after his meetup, and she hadn't gotten a text or a call from him. He must be with Becca, and even if he wasn't, did she want to be with him? She'd finally opened up to someone and look at what happened.

She tried to convince herself, at least she was no longer a virgin. She'd finally been there and done that. Mable shook her head at her own musings. She no longer believed that sex was a dream killer. Her mom had been wrong about that. Love was the problem, that was the dream killer. Even though she'd only been with Ethan for a short time, the pretend family life they had been living had let her start dreaming about what life could be like with a true partner.

Growing up with a dad who was gone for work so much, she hadn't experienced parents who were both partners and co-parents. She'd always felt as if she'd been raised by a single mom. Other kids and even teachers had assumed her parents were divorced because of her dad's schedule. Distracted by her thoughts, she'd walked past Pupcakes and Clawssants to the corner of Main Street and Railway Avenue. She stood waiting for the light, and Iggy yipped and tugged on her lead.

"Sorry about that, Iggy," Mable said. She turned around and walked back to Kate's store. She looked in the bakery, checking to see if Ethan was there. When it was clear he wasn't inside, she didn't know if she was relieved or sad. She pushed open the door. Kate looked up from the bakery case she was reloading and smiled.

"Hi, Mable, and Ms. Iggy!"

"Hi Kate, how's everything going?"

"You would not believe how many new clients have found me since the parade the other day! I've got a bunch of new social media followers, and I've been running out of dog treats."

"I'm so happy to hear that!"

"I really can't thank you and Ethan enough."

Iggy barked.

Kate came around the corner with a treat and knelt. "Paw," she said.

Iggy put up her paw, and Kate shook it. "Thank you so much, Iggy! You were the hit of the parade!"

Kate gave Iggy the treat, and she gobbled it up. "Where's Ethan tonight?"

Mable's face fell. "H-he ah, I'm not sure."

"Oh no, did you two break up?" Kate frowned.

If Kate hadn't had such a look of genuine concern, Mable would have nodded and said it was no big deal. Kate's face mirrored Mable's surprise and sadness so that Mable couldn't hold back her tears.

Kate ran to the counter and got a couple of tissues for Mable; she handed them to Mable, who wiped her eyes and blew her nose. Kate patted Mable's back, making small circles as Mable cried.

"Honey, I'm so sorry. Do you want to talk? Did he do something he shouldn't have? Come sit down and talk. Unless you don't want to?"

Mable walked over to the table and sat down.

Kate went to the front door and flipped over the sign to say Closed.

Mable got up. "I don't want to take up your time. You need to be open to customers."

"Please stay. How about if we talk, and if I see someone come up to the door, I'll go see what they need?"

Mable sniffed. "He's getting back together with his ex."

Kate's jaw dropped, and she shook her head. "I'm shocked. The way he looked at you, he was so smitten. It doesn't make sense. He didn't look like someone who was still holding on to feelings for someone else."

"I didn't think so, but what do I know?" She looked over at Kate. "I haven't dated much, and after this experience, I think I should go right back to not putting myself out there. I've got a big year ahead, and I don't need the headaches of being with someone."

Kate folded and unfolded a Post-it note she'd taken out of her pocket. "I wish I had some words of wisdom about how it's better to have loved and lost than never have loved at all and all that, but my girlfriend cheated on me with her ex-boyfriend while I was working on getting this place ready to open. My plan for this year is to focus on my business."

"Maybe we should start a no-dating support group?" Mable said.

Kate chuckled. "We are too young to be this cynical about love."

Mable looked Kate up and down. She knew Kate was at least ten years older than her.

"Okay, fine, you're too young to be this cynical about love."

"My mom always said I was born old," Mable said.

"You must be the oldest child."

"Yep." Mable nodded.

Kate pointed to herself. "Same here."

"Maybe we need a cynical oldest child support group."

"Now you are talking," Kate said. "Can I get you a drink of water or pop?"

"Actually, I was going to get a slice of pizza from around the corner. I've got to get back to work on my project."

"That's right, Ethan told me you had a very important paper and presentation you were in the midst of." Kate stood up and threw the Post-it in the trash. "Take what I am saying with a grain of salt, but when I think about how Ethan's face lit up every time he said your name, it's hard for me to believe he'd toss that aside to go back to his ex."

Mable hugged Kate. "You are so sweet. I'm going to stop in here next week, and we can plan our first support group meeting for grumpy oldest siblings."

Kate hugged Mable back, "You've got a deal. Let me get you a bag of treats for Iggy."

Mable pulled out her wallet to pay.

Kate waved her off. "Consider this bag of treats Iggy's sales commission."

"Are you sure?"

"Definitely. Now, good luck with your project!" Kate bent down and gave Iggy one last pat on the head. She handed Mable the bag of grain-free treats and then unlocked the door.

"Thanks for everything, Kate!"

"Anytime, honey."

Mable left the store and continued toward Best Pizza Near Me. It was a Tuesday afternoon just before the start of school, and the streets were empty. Everyone must either be at work or on that last summer vacation before school started next week. Next week, she'd be attending her first staff meeting as a school psychologist intern. Butterflies fluttered in her stomach. She could do this; she could turn off the feelings floating around in her heart and focus on her life's work.

"We've got this, Iggy!"

Yip! Yip!

"Good girl." Mable made a mental note to ask Sean and Nicole if she could take Iggy out on walks after school. She'd be right by their house when she worked at Ida. B. Wells Elementary School. A lump formed in her throat when she thought about going back to her hot, tiny bedroom alone next week.

Chapter Twenty-Nine

♥

Ethan picked up his phone. He had a text from Donnie.

DONNIE: Are you coming to book club tonight?

ETHAN: Shoot, I forgot! Does it matter that I didn't finish the book?

DONNIE: As long as you don't mind possible spoilers, you are more than welcome

ETHAN: Cool, then I'll be there. Do you have time to talk after book club?

DONNIE: Sure, Bastian is spending the night at a friend's, so I don't have to rush home.

ETHAN: Last blast of summer before back to school, huh?

DONNIE: I'm not looking forward to waking that kid up at six a.m. come next week.

ETHAN: I hear ya.

DONNIE: See ya soon.

Ethan opened the library app on his phone. He'd been frozen in a loop of thinking about calling Mable and being afraid to call Mable since Monday night. Advice and a push from Donnie to do something, might be just what he needed. He couldn't stay stuck like this. For now, maybe he could distract himself with the book club selection. When he'd borrowed the audio from the library the day the boys left for Atlanta, he'd listened to the first couple of chapters and remembered that he'd liked the start of the book. That seemed like a lifetime ago.

If he listened to the book club book at twice the speed, maybe it would hold his interest and distract him from thoughts of Mable. Plus, he could finish it before heading over to Books and Breads. He pressed play and started listening. Brownie Book Club was devoted to cozy mysteries, and this month's book was the first in the Mad Potter Series. It was called *Kil'n Time*. He needed to stop thinking about Mable. His stomach clenched. He'd really messed things up by agreeing to talk with Becca. Just thinking about how she'd expected him to drop everything and run off with her made him want to punch a wall. Instead of that, he added minutes to his timer and picked up the jump rope.

After a punishing workout and an afternoon moving the furniture around his room, Ethan was on his way to the book club. He'd earned one of Donnie's signature s'mores brownies, not only because he'd burned over five hundred calories but also because he finished the book. Too bad he didn't feel like eating.

He pulled the minivan into a spot near Books and Breads and parked. He walked down the block to Donnie's door and pulled it open. The smell of freshly brewed coffee and brownies hit him in the face. He frowned. He wished Mable were here. She would have liked the book, and he knew she never passed up a warm-from-the-oven brownie. Donnie was standing and talking with an older woman. He looked up when the door chimed and waved Ethan over. Ethan walked over to Donnie and the woman.

"Glad you could make it!" Donnie said.

"I even finished the book."

"Well done!" Donnie said, "Ethan, have you met Nancy Werner?"

Ethan put his hand out. "No, I don't think I have. Nice to meet you, Nancy."

"Nice to meet you too, Ethan," Nancy said, shaking his hand.

"Ethan, you might be seeing a lot of Nancy soon," Donnie said.

Ethan cocked his head. "How so?"

"Do you have children, Ethan? I'm a school secretary at Ida. B. Wells Elementary."

Ethan pointed to himself, "I don't have kids, but I'm the manny for Franklin and Liam Belmont."

"Oh yes, the mayor's twins! Wow, they're already going to kindergarten. Time flies."

"It sure does. Sebastian is starting sophomore year next week," Donnie said.

Nancy shook her head. It seems like he was at Ida B. Wells just yesterday. She pushed her chin-length blonde hair behind her ears. "These kids keep getting older, but me and you still look like we are twenty-five. Right, Donnie?"

"Exactly," Donnie said and smiled. He clapped his hands together and looked around the bakery's seating area. "Looks like we have a full house. You two help yourselves to a brownie and coffee, tea, or water. We'll be starting shortly." Donnie walked away to assist someone who was standing by the bookstore checkout.

A woman wearing glasses waved at Nancy. Nancy turned to Ethan. "It was nice to meet you, Ethan. I'll see you at the school this fall."

"I hope I won't be in the office too much," Ethan grinned.

"Indeed!" Nancy said and walked over to sit with her friend.

Someone tapped Ethan on the shoulder, and his heart leaped for a moment. He thought it was Mable. He wheeled around to see Jax.

"Dang, bro, you don't have to look so bummed to see me," Jax said.

"I'm sorry. I wasn't sure you were going to be here tonight." Ethan said.

"Cozy Mysteries are probably my favorite genre, and Donnie's brownies are definitely my favorite dessert."

"I bet they'd be great with one of the stouts from Hop's Heaven."

"For real. Remind me to talk to Donnie about taking book club on the road to Hop's Heaven," Jax said.

"He could do a whole book fair for grownups thing," Ethan said.

"I love it."

"Let's go sit down."

Ethan and Jax sat down at a table. "Did you finish the book?" Jax asked.

"I listened to the audio. I finished about an hour ago."

"Did you guess who the killer was?" Jax leaned in to ask Ethan quietly.

"I thought it was her sister at first, but then at the very end, I was sure it was the assistant," Ethan said. "I might have figured it out, but I've been too distracted over Mable to concentrate on much of anything."

"I didn't guess either," Jax said. "And don't run off when book club is over. We need to talk about the other night."

Donnie was walking up to the front of the room now with the book in his hand.

Ethan leaned over to whisper, "Can't say I want to rehash the Becca thing, but I want to talk with you and Donnie afterward. I need help."

"Sure thing," Jax said.

Donnie smiled widely. "Folks, we have a full house here tonight! Thanks so much for coming out for Brownie Book Club. How many of you read *Kil'n Time?*" Only a few hands weren't raised. "And how many of you guessed who the killer was?" No one raised their hands. "Fantastic! Let's start off by going around the room and sharing your name and who you thought was the killer."

Two and a half hours later, the last stragglers left Books and Breads. Jax and Ethan helped Donnie clean up from the club meeting, and then they all sat down with a cold beer.

Ethan looked at his beer. A lump had formed in his throat. Would his friends think he was an idiot? Could he make amends to Mable? "Thanks for having time for me," he managed to get out.

"Of course, Ethan, that's what friends are for." Jax said.

"I'm happy to share any advice I can, but I'm rusty. I've only gone out on a few dates since Maggie died," Donnie said. Jax patted Donnie's hand.

"So, what happened with Mable?" Jax asked.

Ethan started from the pet parade and brought Donnie and Jax up to date.

"Let me get this straight, and this might sound a little crass. Practically right after you two had sex for the first time, you told her your ex was in town and you needed to meet up with her," Donnie said.

Ethan hung his head.

Jax just shook their head.

"Basically," Ethan said.

"And now you realize how dumb you were."

"You've hit the nail on the head," Ethan said. "And to make things worse, how can I say this?"

"There's more? Tell me you didn't do anything with Becca," Jax said.

"God, no, nothing like that. We only talked, and that didn't last long."

"And since you saw Becca and told her you wanted nothing to do with her, you haven't tried to call or text Mable?" Donnie asked.

"Right."

"Okay, tell us what makes things worse," Jax said and took a drink of beer.

"She didn't have much experience when we got together."

Donnie's brows lowered in thought.

Jax sighed. "Geez, Ethan."

Ethan's face flushed. "I know."

"I don't think it does you any good for me and Jax to tell you how foolish you were. I'm sure you know that you might have lost an exceptional woman forever. I bet it is eating you alive," Donnie said.

"I can't get her out of my head. I know I managed to listen to the book today, but shit, that was only because I knew I was coming here and you two could help me from drowning."

"You should have told us what was going on as soon as Becca texted you. We could have set you straight before you blew things up with Mable," Jax said.

"I feel like I'm going to puke," Ethan moaned and laid his head on the table.

"Take some slow breaths. We are going to help you fix this—as much as we can," Donnie said as he patted Ethan on the back.

"You need to contact Mable. If you're afraid to call her, then send a voice message. Don't just text her." Jax said.

"Okay, okay," Ethan said. "What should I say?"

"I'd start by saying you're sorry, you told Becca off, and you would very much like to talk with her in person, whenever and wherever she'd like to meet."

"I can do that. Do you think it will work?"

Donnie stroked his beard in thought. "If she agrees to meet you, you have to take baby steps and show Mable you are worthy of her trust. I think you two had the start of something great. Aside from the fact that you are a foot shorter than me—"

"Hey!" Ethan interjected.

"Aside from the height difference, you two remind me of me and Maggie." Donnie choked on his wife's name.

Jax's eyes were glossy, and they patted Donnie on the shoulder.

Ethan swallowed hard. "Gosh, man," was all he could say.

"Do you think it's too late to call now?"

"If she's like me, she'll let you go to voicemail," Jax said.

"Good point," Donnie said.

"Well, I won't get my hopes up. I've got to call before I lose my nerve. I'm going to go outside and do it right now. You two stay here."

"Ten-four," Jax said.

Ethan walked outside and paced. *Speak from the heart,* Ethan; *it's all you can do.* He unlocked his phone and clicked on his contacts. Mable was pinned at the top alongside Sean and Mayor Devin. He put in his earbuds and pressed call.

Ring

Ring

Ring

Ring

"You've reached Mable Weaverton," her message began. He was glad that at least she hadn't blocked his calls.

Beep

"Hi, it's Ethan. Please keep listening! I'm so sorry I didn't call you sooner. I was just a craven asshole. I completely screwed up and if I could go back in time to Saturday and fix things, I would do it in a heartbeat, even if the exchange was a couple of decades of my life. Can we talk? I can meet you whenever and wherever is best for you. And please tell Iggy I miss her, too."

Ethan's hand shook as he ended the call. Sweat was beading on his forehead. He took a breath and held it for a moment, trying to calm himself down. Donnie wouldn't be happy if he threw up on his newly mopped floor. He opened the door and walked back to his friends.

"How did it go?" Jax asked.

"I left a message."

"How many times did the phone ring before you got voicemail?" Donnie asked.

"Four."

"At least she didn't block you then," Jax said.

"That's what I thought too," Ethan said. "How long do you think it might be before she calls me back?"

Donnie blew out a breath. "Hard to say. Could be she calls you back tonight, and that could be good or bad."

Ethan's face drooped. "I didn't even consider she might call me back to tell me to screw off."

Jax patted Ethan's hand. "I can't say anything for sure, but I don't think she'd call you back and tell you to drop dead."

"Thanks?"

"Sorry," Jax said. "You're just going to have to wait and see, sit in your discomfort for at least a few days. Whatever you do, don't call her again. You don't want to come off like you have stalker tendencies. No one wants to deal with that."

Ethan put his face in his hands. "All I can do now is hope."

Donnie and Jax nodded in agreement.

Chapter Thirty

♥

Mable had done it. She'd finished editing her presentation. It was time to celebrate, so she turned on *Bluey* for Iggy and did a happy dance around the house. She bent down and tried to high-five Iggy, but that wasn't happening. Too bad Ethan wasn't around. She knew he'd have been all in to help her celebrate. He'd be wrapping her in one of his bear hugs and then his soft lips would be on hers. She sighed. Mable went back into the bedroom and sent her presentation off to Susan to review. Once that was complete, she flopped down on the guest bed and texted Hannah.

MABLE: Finished my project for now. You busy tonight?

HANNAH: Yay for being done, boo for going out.

MABLE: Crap, I was hoping we could hang out.

HANNAH: Sorry, I took a catering job tonight.

MABLE: (crying face emoji)

HANNAH: (blowing a kiss emoji)

Mable closed out of her text app and then scrolled through her social media for a while. She couldn't stop herself from looking for Ethan, but his profile was private. Rolling over onto her stomach, she clicked on her voicemail. Once again she pressed play and listened to the message Ethan had left a couple of days ago. Mable recited the words as they played. She knew what Hannah would have to say about that. If you've listened to his message so many times that you have it memorized, you should just call him. Stop torturing yourself! That's exactly what Hannah would say, and it was also almost the same advice she'd given Sean when he'd started dating Nicole.

Mable bit her bottom lip. Now he was waiting longer to hear from her than she had waited after he met with his ex. She hadn't done it on purpose, but what if he thought she was that petty? She replayed the message. Would this be the night she finally called him back? It was the crack in his voice when he asked her to tell Iggy hi that did her in. She knew she was going to give him another chance. It was just a matter of when. She'd been waiting until she'd finished her project and now that was in Susan's hands. Her hands shook as she took a deep breath and pressed the call button under Ethan's message. She hoped he answered because if she got his voicemail; she was going to hang up.

Ring

Ring

Mable stood up and paced the room. *Come on, Ethan, answer the phone.*

"Mable, hi," Ethan said panting.

"Did I catch you at a bad time?"

"No, not, at, all." Big breaths filled the space between each of his words.

"Are you at the gym or something? I can call back," Mable said.

"I was running," he said. His breath was almost back to normal.

"Where were you running?"

"This sounds ridiculous, but I'm just a couple of blocks from Sean and Nicole's."

"Just like when I called you in a panic almost two weeks ago," Mable said.

"I swear, it's just a total coincidence."

"Right, okay, sure it is," Mable teased.

"No, for real, it's just because it's a nice four-mile loop."

"Here I was thinking you missed me."

She could hear Ethan clear his throat, and when he spoke, his voice was thick. "I missed you so much."

"I missed you too, Ethan, but I was also, and am still, sad and hurt."

"I was a real jerk," he said.

"Beyond a doubt."

"How can I make it up to you?"

"It might take weeks, months even," Mable said.

"I'm down for that, even if it takes years."

"Really?"

"Yes, one hundred percent," Ethan said

"How close are you to the house?"

"I can be there in five minutes if I walk."

"Then how about you run on over here."

"On my way," he said.

Mable hung up the phone and rushed to throw on a fresh shirt and deodorant. She walked to the bathroom to get her brush. She felt so light, she was surprised her feet were touching the ground. Mable stood in the living room looking out the window and brushing her hair. When she saw Ethan turn the corner onto her block, she threw down the brush and walked outside.

Ethan sprinted the rest of the way to her door. He stopped on the front porch step. His tank top and shorts clung to him, and he paused to take a long drink from his water bottle.

Mable watched him, cataloging his wet curls, the outline of his abs through his shirt, and those finely muscled thighs of his. "Is this the start of you making up with me?"

"Is it working?" he asked.

"You did sprint here when I asked. I think that's a good start."

"Do you want to come in and talk?" she asked, and then she put up her hands. "Just talk. We aren't at a kissing or otherwise place of forgiveness yet."

"I'd love to talk. I'll wait as long as it takes to earn kissing and stuff." He grinned and cocked an eyebrow.

"You better," she said, and she took him by the hand and led him into the house.

The moment Ethan walked across the threshold; Iggy was yipping away, clamoring for his attention. "Iggy! I missed you too!" he said. He toed off his shoes and knelt to pet Iggy. She jumped up and clawed at his chest. "Oh, honey," he picked her up and held her in his arms like a baby and gave her belly rubs.

"I'm not sure which one of us missed you more."

"Does Iggy have you beat?" Ethan asked shyly.

"No way," Mable said. "I'll be right back." She walked into the main bedroom and came back and handed Ethan the same shirt of Sean's Ethan had borrowed that first night.

"Is this déjà vu, or am I getting a redo?"

"I don't think forgetting the past does us any good. Plus nights—like the tornado warning night—aren't something I ever want to forget."

Ethan stripped off his shirt. Mable licked her lips, unable to pull her eyes away from his flat stomach and the V that his obliques made. His running shorts were slung low on his hips, and she had to clench her thighs to stop the throbbing that started.

Ethan put on the long shirt, and Mable regained her composure. "I'll get us some water, and we can sit and chat." Iggy pranced over to the couch and jumped right up onto it.

"Water would be great," Ethan said.

Mable got a couple of glasses of water and walked over to the couch where Ethan was giving Iggy more belly rubs.

"Here you go."

"Thanks."

Mable watched as Ethan gulped down the whole glass of water. Once he set it down, she asked if he'd like another.

"I'm good for now."

"Ready to talk?" she said.

"I'm ready to apologize like no man has ever apologized before."

"Great, I can't wait to hear it." She sat down next to him and folded her hands.

"This isn't an excuse, but I want to explain why I thought I had to talk to Becca the other day. I've already told you about our breakup, but I didn't tell you about why it completely wrecked me."

"Tell me now, I'm listening."

"My dad left me and my mom the summer before junior high."

"Ugh, that does a number on kids," Mable said.

"I know, believe me, I know. After my dad left, my mom spiraled into a deep depression. There were days when I was afraid to go home. She would just sit at the kitchen table in the same clothes she'd had on for several days. She didn't eat, she wasn't sleeping, and I couldn't fix it. I kept calling my dad, begging him to come home, and he stopped answering my phone calls."

"What a dick."

"I know. Well, you know he's not good at fathering. That's something Sean and I have in common."

"True, I was surprised everyone was cordial at the wedding," Mable said.

"It's been rough, but he's made some progress, and we have a pretty decent relationship now, and that is something I never thought would happen the summer he left us."

"As things went on, my mom lost her job; she didn't leave the house for weeks at a time. I think if school had been in session, someone might have called social services."

"I'm so sorry you went through such a tough time."

"Thank you. Gosh, you are just the best person, Mable. I'm so lucky you are even talking to me."

Mable's cheeks pinked.

"That summer was bleak. Suddenly, my dad was gone, and my mom was barely there. When Becca left me, I know this is overused, but I truly had PTSD; only now I was my mom."

Mable reached over and patted Ethan's hand. He took her hand, and she laced her fingers through his.

"I guess my point with that story is that I didn't have healthy relationship models when I was growing up. Everything was fine when I was a little kid, but when they split up. I had a front-row seat to so much depression and dysfunction. Part of me learned that if you can't function after a break-up, then it wasn't really love."

Mable nodded and gave his hand a squeeze.

"When we met, it was so easy and fun. You take my freaking breath away, Mable. On the pet parade float, I could feel myself falling in love with you. Then Becca showed up, and I started thinking I must not be in love because love is gut-wrenching and it breaks you."

"Oh, baby," Mable said.

"So, I said I'd meet her, even though it was breaking my heart to hurt you, and I dreaded seeing her more than I looked forward to it. I met her at Hop's Heaven because I didn't feel right being anywhere alone with her, plus it gave me time to talk with Jax beforehand."

"What advice did Jax give you?"

"Jax told me Becca was an ass and I should not meet her."

"Jax is good people, great head on their shoulders," Mable said.

Ethan nodded. "But I didn't listen. Maybe if she'd been late, I would have come to my senses, but she came on time. She walked into Hop's Heaven as if her presence was doing the place a favor."

Mable snorted.

"You know why she came to Marley Creek?"

"She missed you?"

Ethan threw back his head and laughed. "No, because her family missed me!"

"What?"

"Yeah, they have a beach house on Lake Michigan and spend most of their summers there, and apparently this summer they've spent a lot of time talking about fun times we had at the beach house over the last few years and how it wasn't the same without me there."

"So she was jealous?"

"Bingo. She didn't want me. I really fell for it." Ethan said. Mable shook her head.

"I second-guessed my feelings for you and hurt you. I was willing to put myself back into a relationship with someone who, I now think, never really loved me. I know I broke your trust, and the worst part is, I worry you can't trust me. I'm afraid to trust myself," he said.

Ethan's eyes were glossy, and Mable's chest ached. Her eyes were stinging, and she blinked quickly, trying to stop tears from falling. Iggy jumped down from the couch, and that allowed Mable to move closer to Ethan. She put her hand on his cheek, and he tilted his head, rubbing against her hand.

"I've never been in love before. I've never felt that the risk was worth it," Mable said. The corners of Ethan's mouth turned down. She moved her hand and placed it on his chest. She could feel his heart beating rapidly. "I want to take it day-by-day. I need my space, but I also need you to show me you love me."

Ethan nodded, his eyes brimming with tears. She reached up and brushed away his tears. He leaned in toward her. She looked down at his soft, full lips, and then back up to his eyes. She saw her love reflected back at her.

"I love you, and I'm going to work hard to always be the man you deserve," Ethan said.

He kissed her softly, and she moaned as his tongue pressed between her lips. She opened her mouth, eager for his taste. He pulled her to him, and she straddled his lap. He wrapped her in his arms as they continued to kiss. She could feel the effect she was having on him, and she slowly rocked her hips. Now he was moaning into their kiss.

"Baby, I know it was only a few days, but damn, I missed you," he said.

Their foreheads touched, and she closed her eyes. "The past few days have lasted decades," she said.

"Are you free tomorrow?"

"Susan's going to give me feedback on my project, and I'll need to make changes. I imagine I'll be done by three or four. Why, what's up?"

"Would you go on a date with me?"

"A date?"

"Yes, date number one of many in which I worship you, as you should be worshiped," he said.

"I do deserve that sort of treatment, don't I?"

He picked up her hand and kissed it, and a shiver ran down her back. "What time should I be ready?"

"I'll pick you up at five."

"What should I wear?"

Ethan tilted his head. "Comfortable shoes and you'll probably want to have pockets."

"Comfy shoes and pockets. That's intriguing."

"I'll text you some emoji hints about our date tomorrow," he said.

Mable grinned widely. "This is so fun! Is this what I have to look forward to with you?"

Ethan nodded and looked serious. "This is just the beginning. Now I'd better get going. You have a busy day tomorrow."

Mable got up and walked him to the door. She thought she'd be disappointed that he wasn't going to stay the night, but she liked the effort Ethan was putting into winning her back. *I'm being wooed.* Butterflies filled her stomach.

Chapter Thirty-One

♥

Ethan woke up feeling more refreshed than he could ever remember. "Mable loves me," he said to the empty room. He jumped out of bed and went to the kitchen to make himself a cup of coffee. It was eight a.m., a good time to send his first date hint to Mable.

> ETHAN: You won't mind these claws.

He hit send. *She's never going to guess where we're going from that clue.*

He peeled a couple of boiled eggs for breakfast and thought about Mable and what else he could do today to make this date unforgettable. He should have asked her if she was a flowers kind of girl. Ethan thought back over their time together in his mind. Aside from his idiocy over Becca, there was one other time when they were together when he felt he hadn't put Mable first. When they'd had sex last week and he'd asked her how it was, she'd said fine.

Ethan shook his head. The fact that he'd had to ask her how it was should have been his first clue that it hadn't been very good for her. He didn't know if they would have sex tonight and he didn't care. He was just happy to be with Mable. But if it could happen, he wanted to make sure it was better for her. He pulled out his laptop, opened it, and went to Google. He typed in 'how to make sex better for a virgin.' The search results came back and he clicked a link that looked promising. Suddenly, porn started autoplaying.

"Oh, shit!" Ethan said and slammed his laptop shut. His heart was beating in his throat. Good thing he hadn't used the computer in the Belmont's study. He opened the laptop back up, and the video started playing again! He exited out of the screen, and multiple screens started popping up, all playing various scenes of people having sex. Great, now he had malware. That was going to be a problem for another day. He put the laptop away.

Ethan picked up his phone and texted Donnie.

> ETHAN: Can I call you? Need Advice.

> DONNIE: Sure.

Ethan called, and Donnie picked it up right away. "Hey, buddy, what's up?"

"I need advice. It's a kind of personal."

"Sure, hold on."

Ethan heard voices and laughter, and the muffled sounds of Donnie walking.

"Okay, go ahead."

"You sound like you're not at home. I don't want to bother you. I can figure something else out."

"I'm at lunch with Sebastian. We went out for a bike ride this morning, and now we're getting food. I thought this could be a nice father-son bonding day. I hardly ever take Saturdays off. He's been glued to his phone since we sat down. Tell me what's going on?" Donnie said.

"Okay, good, because it's about sex. Mable and I are going out tonight and, well, I don't think I was a very good partner when we had sex for the first time, and I need advice."

"I'm glad you called; everyone should have good sex."

"Cool, so what do you think? How can I make it good for her?"

Donnie asked a few questions and gave Ethan advice that was centered on lots of foreplay, and recommended a couple of different lubes. Ethan got off the phone with Donnie, feeling better about how he could give Mable as much pleasure as he'd enjoyed when they'd had sex. According to Donnie, CVS Pharmacy carried the best lube, so he got in the minivan and off he went. When he was in the pharmacy, he saw a container of cotton candy. He took a picture of that and sent it as clue number two to Mable.

He picked up some bottled water and got a bag of keto chips; he felt nervous going up to the counter with just a container of lube. At least the CVS wasn't right on Main Street in Marley Creek. He was sure if that was the case, he'd run into someone he knew. Once he was back home, he packed a bag to keep in the car, just in case Mable invited him to spend the night. He checked his watch and sent another hint to Mable. This one would probably give the game away, but that was okay. He wanted her to guess before he got there.

> ETHAN: If you give me a whirl, I'll make sure we don't tilt.

Ethan put his phone in his pocket and locked the door to the house. He walked over to the car, got in and drove over to Sean and Nicole's.

When he was standing on the doorstep, he looked at his phone. Mable had texted back three emojis: a roller coaster, a carousel horse, and a ticket. Ethan grinned; she'd figured it out.

Mable opened the door. She was wearing her hair in two braids. She had on a pair of denim overalls over a tube top. Ethan licked his lips, and before he could speak, Mable threw the door open and flung herself into his arms. He turned her to the side and dipped her. She gasped with delight and his chest expanded. Ethan kissed her, and then he pulled her up and they kissed again. He deepened the kiss, and she invited his tongue into her mouth. He squeezed her tight. The door had shut behind Mable when she'd come out, and now Iggy was scratching the screen door and barking.

Mable pulled back, "I think Iggy is jealous."

Ethan turned to face the door. He rubbed Mable's back, unable to stop touching her. "What if we promise to bring her back a stuffed toy?"

Mable said, "You hear that, Iggy? Uncle Ethan is going to bring you back a new toy!"

Ethan nodded.

Mable put her hand on her hip. "But you're going to win me the big prize, right?"

Ethan kissed the tip of Mable's nose. "I'm going to win you a stuffed animal as big as me."

"Good," Mable said. "Let me grab my purse and I'll be right back."

"I'll go out to the car if that's okay with you," he said.

"I love that you are such a gentleman," she said.

Ethan floated on air as he went to the minivan. She said love. He would never tire of her saying she loved something he did.

***

Mable ran up to the door and danced around as she unlocked it. She'd drank one too many lemon shake-ups at the carnival. She opened the door and ignored Iggy's barking as she rushed to the bathroom. As soon as her bladder was blissfully empty, she walked to the living room where Ethan was now sharing the couch with the little dog and a giant blue octopus.

"It seemed like a great idea, but now I'm questioning having a six-foot-long octopus in my tiny bedroom."

Ethan laughed and nervously ran a hand through his hair. "Whoops."

Mable walked over and sat on Ethan's lap. She leaned down and kissed him gently on the mouth. "You taste like cotton candy," she said.

"So do you," he said and bit down gently on her bottom lip.

Heat rushed to her core. He put his hand between her thighs, and she shifted, trying to move his hand closer to where she wanted his touch. "What would you say if I told you I think I'd like to try sex again?"

Ethan swallowed loudly. "I would say I'm ready to make it so good for you."

Mable moved off his lap and stood, holding her hand out. "Well, then."

"I've just got to run out to the car and get my bag."

Mable cocked her eyebrow. "You brought a bag of tricks?"

Ethan blush "Only treats for you."

"Then you'd better hurry," Mable said.

Ethan was back in the house in record time. He dropped his bag on the floor next to the couch and pulled Mable into his arms. Butterflies were fluttering in her stomach, but this time it was excitement, not fear. She moved her hand to unsnap her overalls.

Ethan put one hand on her hip and with the other, he moved to stop her from unsnapping. "Can I?"

Mable nodded. Ethan unclipped each side of her overalls, and they fell to the ground. A shiver ran through her, and Ethan paused.

"Is everything okay?"

"More than okay," she said. Her voice was husky. He placed his hands on each side of her face and kissed her softly. She leaned into the kiss, putting her hands on his chest, feeling the muscles underneath his button-down shirt. His tongue slid into her mouth, and he moved his hand to the nape of her neck, pushing her closer to him. She needed him closer to her, too. The scent of Ethan was short-circuiting her brain. She craved skin-to-skin contact. She pulled on his shirt, untucking it, and then her trembling hands were unbuttoning his shirt.

"Can I help?" Ethan asked.

"God, yes, help me," she said.

He quickly unbuttoned his shirt, and Mable moved it off his shoulders and it fell to the floor. She ran her hands over his chest, moving down to his waist. She unbuttoned his pants and reached in, unable to wait much longer. "You're like marble, hard and smooth." She gripped him, her hand barely able to wrap around all of him.

He moaned, "Mable."

"Yes?"

"I love..." he said, and she felt him thrusting into her touch. "...what you are doing, but tonight is about you having sex that feels good."

She shifted, her panties wet now. "Making you moan turns me on." She stroked him again, and then she took his hand and put it in her panties.

"You're so wet," he said, gasping.

"Mm-hmm," she said.

He slipped a finger into her wet pussy and moved it in and out. "Can I taste your sweet pussy?"

She nodded, and he scooped her up into his arms. She giggled into his neck. Even though she was taller than him, he had a way of making her feel small and delicate.

He placed her on the bed, and then he was on his knees genuflecting. He put her leg over her shoulder.

"Kiss me, Ethan," she said.

Her legs quivered as he began kissing the sensitive skin behind her knee. She failed to suppress a giggle.

"Does that tickle?" he murmured against her skin.

"Yes, baby," she said. He kissed and licked her leg, inching closer to her center. She was aching with need. "Ethan, I need your tongue," she begged.

Finally, his tongue swirled around her swollen nub. "Oh my god," Mable said. She grabbed his hair, directing him. He took her clit into his mouth and sucked. She moved her head from side to side, feeling the building pressure. As if he could read her mind, he worked a second finger into her pussy. She tightened her muscles around his fingers and thrilled as he moaned her name.

"Fuck, you are so tight," he said.

She was bearing down on his hand and his tongue picked up the pace, matching her as she rocked.

"Let go, Mable, I'm here with you."

"I want your cock filling me up, Ethan," she moaned.

He moved back, licking his lips. "Are you sure?"

She ground against him, his thumb circling her clit. "Totally."

He pulled off his shorts and underwear and took a condom and the small tube of lubricant out of his back pocket. Mable leaned up on an elbow. "What's that?"

"I brought some lube to make sure everything feels better for you."

Mable moved over and made room for Ethan on the bed. She put her hand out, "Can I put on the condom?"

Mable watched as his cock twitched. No words were needed. He handed her the condom. She opened it and carefully put it on his rock-hard cock. Once it was secure, he opened the lube and took a small amount, coating two fingers with it. Mable spread her legs, and he pushed his lubed fingers into her. The chill of the lube surprised her, and she squeaked.

Ethan froze. "What's wrong?"

"Nothing, the lube was a little cold."

"I'm sorry."

"Don't be, just fuck me."

"Yes, ma'am," he said. She steeled herself for potential pain, but she felt waves of pleasure as Ethan took care to stroke her nub as he pushed his cock into her wet and well-lubricated pussy inch by inch. She felt her walls make room for his cock and finally he was all in. He continued stroking her as she unclenched her pussy muscles until she felt full, but not sore. "Now, baby," she said. And he carefully slid in and out.

She rocked again, in time with him, and her orgasm building. "This feels so good. This feels so right! Oh, Ethan, yes, harder." She ran her nails down his back, spurring him on as she rode her pleasure. It felt like she was about to dive off a cliff, and it was so much better than those days alone in her bedroom with her bullet, Rex.

"God, Mable, you're so fucking perfect," Ethan shouted, and she was done crashing over the top. She wished she could stay in this moment with Ethan forever.

When they were finished, Ethan looked at her wide-eyed, and she imagined she looked the same. "Damn," was all she could say.

"Damn, indeed," he said.

Chapter Thirty-two

The insistent sound of a phone ringing woke Ethan. He rolled over and checked his phone. Nothing. He gave Mable a loving shove.

"Mable, baby, your phone is ringing."

"Let it go to voicemail," she mumbled into the pillow.

"Fine by me," Ethan spooned Mable and closed his eyes.

Less than thirty seconds later, Mable's phone began ringing again.

"Okay, fine," Mable said, throwing back the covers and sitting up. She pulled her phone off the charger and rubbed her eyes. "Shit, it's Sean and Nicole."

"Better answer it then."

Mable unlocked her phone. "Hey Sean! What's up?" She said into the phone, and then she whispered to Ethan, "I'm going to put him on speaker."

Ethan gave her a thumbs-up. He lay back down to listen.

"When we got to the airport, the craziest thing happened. They were able to switch us to a direct flight."

"And we got upgraded to first class!" Nicole said in the background.

"Wow, that's cool," Mable said.

"We're in an Uber and we'll see you in about half an hour!" Sean said.

"That's, ah, great, guys," Mable said as she shook Ethan. Ethan sat up, and they both stared at each other. Ethan mouthed, "Crap!"

"Tell Iggy we can't wait to see her!"

"I will," Mable said and ended the call.

"They are almost home!"

"I'm glad they called before they got here," Ethan said. "I'll let Iggy out ."

"Great, I'll go clean up the living room. I hope Iggy didn't get a hold of my underwear."

"Good idea. I don't remember where I left my shirt." He looked at her sleep-tousled hair and her cute little nose. He stood up and wrapped his arms around her waist. She leaned down, and they shared a lingering kiss, until Iggy started barking.

"Okay, okay, I'm coming," he said.

He walked out to the patio barefoot. Iggy took off into the yard. She did a couple of laps around the yard before finding a place to pee. Ethan did not know if Mable had said anything to Sean and Nicole about him and their relationship. He hoped Sean would be okay with them dating. He knew Sean thought of Mable as a sister. Maybe someday she'd be his sister-in-law.

He couldn't keep the smile off his face. He was going to do everything he could over the days, weeks, and months to come to earn Mable's trust, and someday he would ask her to marry him. Iggy was trotting around in the backyard, so Ethan reclined on the chaise lounge. He yawned widely; they had kept each other up late last night, and he'd planned on sleeping in. He thought about how gorgeous Mable looked beneath him and how he couldn't wait to taste her again.

"Ethan!" Mable yelled, and his eyes flew open.

"Are they here?"

"Not yet. Were you sleeping?" Mable said.

"I was just resting my eyes?"

"Where's Iggy?"

Ethan stood up and scanned the yard, "She was right over…"

"I don't see her!" Mable's voice was rising.

They both ran down the deck steps and into the backyard. "Iggy!" Mable yelled.

"Iggy, come here, Iggy!" Ethan yelled. He ran over to the fence. "Oh my God, do you think?"

Mable rushed over to Ethan. Her eyes were wide. She pulled her hair away from her face.

"Did she get out of the yard?"

Ethan put his face in his hands. "Fuck, this is bad."

Mable put her hand on Ethan's shoulder, "We can't panic; we've got to figure it out. She can't have gone that far."

Ethan wrapped an arm around Mable. "I'm going to call the police non-emergency number."

"Should we get in the car and drive around or canvass the neighborhood?"

"Can you call Hannah and Kate? Maybe Iggy would sniff her way to Main Street?" Ethan said as he dialed the phone.

"Oh my God, she is so tiny. What if, no, I can't even say it."

"Don't say it!" Ethan said to Mable and then, "Hello, I need to report a missing dog."

Ethan stayed on the phone for a couple of minutes, answering questions. "Thank you so much for all your help. Oh good, you got the picture. Yes, she is the cutest dog. She's also very smart. Okay, we'll meet you out front."

Ethan ended the call. His heart was racing as he ran through the house. "The police are on their way! Mable, Mable? Where are you at?" He checked the bedrooms and rushed out the front door.

Sitting on the front stoop was Mable and in her arms was Iggy. Ethan gasped. "She's here."

Mable turned to Ethan, wearing a big, sappy grin. Iggy was licking her face. Mable giggled, "I don't even like doggie kisses."

"Where was she? What happened?" Ethan walked over and sat down next to Mable and Iggy.

"I ran out of the house and jogged up and down the block calling for her! I couldn't stop thinking about her trying to cross Main Street to get to Kate's yummy treats.! I didn't see her anywhere! I ran back to the house to tell you we needed to get in the car and go look for her and she was on the porch! Just sitting here, wagging her tail."

"No way."

"I know! Bonkers, right?" Mable wiped her eyes. I've never been so relieved in my life.

"You and me both, except," he paused and gave her a kiss on the crown of her head, "nothing compares to the moment you said you loved me."

"Aww, baby," Mable said. She rested her head on Ethan's chest.

Warmth spread throughout his chest and into his arms and legs. He could sit here with her for the rest of eternity. A beat later he remembered, "Crap! I better call the police back."

Just then, a police car turned onto the street, and right behind them was another car.

"Damn," Mable said. "That's probably Sean and Nicole's Uber."

Ethan and Mable stood up as the police car stopped out front and the other car pulled into the driveway. The back doors of the Uber flew open, and Sean and Nicole ran over to Ethan and Mable. The driver exited the car, shook his head, and unloaded the luggage onto the driveway. Once the trunk was empty, he hopped back into his car and left.

The police officer ambled over to the group. "I see Iggy is back home safe and sound."

"What the heck is going on, Ethan? Mable? Why is Officer Bradley here?" Sean scowled and crossed his arms.

Nicole put her hands out for Iggy. Iggy shook her head and yipped at Nicole. "Oh no, she's forgotten all about us!"

Ethan ignored Sean for a moment and spoke to Officer Bradley. She was a tall Black woman who wore her hair in a short natural style that complimented her heart-shaped face. "Thanks so much for taking the time to come out. Iggy is so smart, she must have realized it wasn't safe for her to be out and about after she dug her way under the fence."

Officer Bradley put her hands in front of herself, palms out. "Do you think I could pet her?" She moved her hand closer to Iggy, who sniffed it politely and then gave her a lick. Officer Bradley tried to repress a giggle and failed. "She is a cutie!" She gave Iggy a goodbye pat on the head and then nodded to the group. "Y'all have a nice rest of your Sunday."

Everyone nodded and waved as Officer Bradley left.

Sean turned to Ethan. "Iggy got out from under the fence?"

"Yes, want me to show you where? If you have some wood, we can cover it now." Ethan and Sean walked over to the garage. Sean picked up a hammer and a box of nails. Ethan looked around for wood.

"I have a small pile of firewood out back that was wooden pallets. We can find a piece or two in the back." Sean said.

Ethan's stomach churned. He waited for Sean to lay into him about Iggy, about Mable. He followed through the side gate and into the backyard.

"I see the firewood. I'll go get a couple of pieces." Ethan jogged over to the wood and wished he could keep jogging out of the yard and back home. He picked up a couple of foot-long pieces and walked over to Sean.

"What's the scoop with you and Mable?" Sean said, holding a hammer.

"We're dating."

"Uh, huh. And you're with her on a Sunday morning because?" Sean's barrel chest had never been intimidating until now.

Ethan gulped. "I spent the night."

Sean scowled at Ethan. "You better know what you are doing, little brother. I won't allow you to hurt Mable."

Ethan winced. *Too Late* but that was the past. "I love her. She's it for me, and I'm going to work every day to be a better man for her."

Sean's scowl dropped. His eyebrows raised. "How long was I gone?"

"Didn't you tell me recently, when you know you know?"

Sean nodded slowly. "That I did. So, when are you two getting hitched?"

"Chill, old man, we are taking things slow. We have plenty of time. We aren't over the hill like you."

"Hi-larious, little brother."

Ethan and Sean worked together and quickly refilled the hole and added the extra wood to make sure Iggy couldn't wiggle under the fence.

They walked around to the front of the house. Nicole was clapping as Iggy danced on her hind legs.

"She's got a lot of tricks up her sleeve to show you two," Mable said.

Ethan walked over and put his arm around Mable's waist.

Sean stood behind Nicole, and she leaned back into him. He wrapped his arms around her.

"Looks like Iggy's greatest trick might be playing matchmaker," Nicole said.

Mable chuckled.

"What's so funny?" Ethan said.

"I thought of a silly joke," Mable said.

"Go on, say it."

"I was going to say good things come in small packages."

Ethan just shook his head. "That was terrible. You need to leave the bad jokes to Sean."

"Hey!" Sean said. "I'm funny."

"Sure, you are." Nicole said patting his arm. "Let's get our luggage inside so we can show Iggy all her presents." Nicole picked up Iggy in her arms, and Iggy gave a happy bark this time. Then they walked to the driveway.

Ethan turned to Mable. "Looks like our days playing house are over. Are you ready to go back into the real world?"

"With you? I can go anywhere if I'm with you," Mable said.

Ethan placed a soft kiss on her lips, sealing the deal.

EPILOGUE

♥

Ethan picked up the painting cloths off the floor and folded them into squares. He looked at the room, admiring how the light lavender color he'd picked out worked so well with the refurbished bedroom furniture he'd gray-washed over the last couple of weeks. It had taken hours and hours, but if he hadn't DIY'd it, he wouldn't have been able to afford the security deposit and first and last month's rent payment for the apartment as well as furnishings.

He walked into the living room and carefully lifted and carried the area rug into the bedroom. He rolled it out and then rubbed the plush, dark gray and white fabric with his hand. Ethan gave in to his temptation and laid down on the rug for a few minutes. He checked his phone. He still had about an hour before he had to pick up the twins from kindergarten. Once homework was done and they were ready for bed, Ethan would be off for the three-day weekend. Thank goodness for parent-teacher conferences.

Ethan had been spending all his free time working on getting the apartment ready, and it would all be worth it when he saw the look on Mable's face. She was going to be so happy when she realized she was finally going to have a place of her own. He loved doing things to make Mable happy. Of course, he admitted he wouldn't miss having to go over to the apartment where Mable currently lived. He'd pack all her stuff with a smile on his face tonight if she'd let him. He sat up and looked at the queen bed. It was nice spending the night in each other's arms, in her twin bed, but it would be nice to roll over without falling out of the bed, especially since when he had fallen out of the bed, he'd woken up Mable's roommate.

Ethan walked through the apartment, checking to make sure everything was perfect for later today. A knock on the door startled Ethan, and then he realized it could only be one person.

"Coming!" he said as he rushed to the door and opened it.

"Stairs are not a super-pregnant lady's friend." Zaina gasped as she held her side.

"Can I get you a glass of water?"

Zaina put her hand on top of her belly, "This child is up in my ribs. I swear she's taking up half of my lung capacity."

"You're having a girl?"

"Jasper and I want to be surprised, but according to the tarot cards, we are having a girl."

"When are you due?"

"December fourteenth."

"Wow, only a couple of months to go."

Zaina winced, "Ouch." She rubbed her side. "I guess she can't wait to meet us because now she's kicking. Do you want to feel her?"

Ethan's eyes got big. "Can I?"

"Sure." Zaina took his hand and put it on her belly.

A moment later, he felt a tiny kick. "That's so cool!" He grinned widely, his brown eyes sparkling.

"Now, if you think that's cool, what do you think about leaving Devin and coming to work for me? Just think about it, a brand-new baby, not those rambunctious boys that you have to wrangle all day."

Ethan laughed and shook his head. "Not a chance."

"A girl's got to try, right?"

"You're going to be a great mom. I promise."

"Thanks, Ethan, that's very kind of you to say." She pressed her fingers to her eyes. "Doggone it. Everything makes me weepy."

"Let me get you a tissue." Ethan rushed to the kitchen counter and pulled a paper towel off the roll. "Erm, make that a paper towel." He said handing Zaina the paper.

Zaina dabbed her eyes, "I just came up here to bring you the spare set of keys and see if I could take a peek to see what you've done with the place." She handed him the keys.

"Thanks again for Jasper's and your help with this—and for leaving the living room furniture and the dinette set. That really helped me save some money."

"As far as I'm concerned, you and Mable are like family. I had lots of great times in this apartment. I know I'm leaving it in excellent hands."

"Now you're making me teary," Ethan said, and he gave her arm a squeeze.

Zaina laughed. "My hormones are contagious."

Ethan gave Zaina a tour of her former apartment, and then it was time to pick up the twins. He walked with Zaina back downstairs and then drove to Ida B. Wells Elementary and got in the pickup line.

***

While he was watching the boys enjoy their thirty minutes of after-school screen time, his phone chimed. Mable texted him.

MABLE: Must stay late and finish five evaluations. Still want to get dinner? Or just pick me up in the morning?

Ethan's stomach dropped. He was so excited to show Mable their new place. He'd been working for a month toward this day.

ETHAN: I don't mind waiting so we can still leave tonight.

MABLE: Late sounds better than Friday night at the apt.

Ethan blew out a sigh of relief so loud Franklin looked up from his game. "Was that you, E?"

"Who else would it be? The mouse in your pocket?"

Franklin dropped his iPad and started jumping up and down. "What mouse? I don't like mice!"

Liam laughed so hard he rolled off the couch with a clunk.

Ethan winced. "Are you okay there, buddy?"

"I'm fwine." Liam said, picking up his iPad and pressing play.

Franklin was on the floor now, his iPad abandoned.

"Franklin, what are you looking for?"

"The mouse you said was in my pocket."

"I'm sorry, buddy. I was just kidding."

"That wasn't very nice," Franklin said.

"You're right." Ethan should have remembered Franklin was a very literal thinker.

He looked at his phone.

ETHAN: Pick you up at eight?

MABLE: Eight it is.

Ethan got up and did a little happy dance. Liam looked up and saw Ethan dancing, so he put down his iPad and started copying his dance moves.

"Are we having a dance party?" asked Liam.

"We sure are," said Ethan.

***

Mable hoped that whatever Ethan had planned for the weekend was low-key. She was exhausted. The moment she got home, she changed out of her dress pants and blouse and put on her favorite sweatpants and Illinois State hoodie. She removed her makeup and braided her hair into a long French braid. When she was ready, she lay on her bed and put in her headphones. She quickly dozed off.

The ringing of her phone sounded in her ears. For a moment, she thought it was her alarm clock going off, signaling the start of a new day. Then she remembered that she'd already finished her workday and had the weekend ahead of her. She swiped to answer the call.

"Hello," she said.

"I'm downstairs. Do you want me to come up or...?" Ethan said.

Mable rolled to a sitting position. "No, you don't have to come up. I can be down in a couple of minutes."

"You have your bag packed, right?."

Mable looked over at the duffle bag that was sitting on her desk. "Yep, are you going to tell me where we are going?"

"You'll know soon, trust me," Ethan said.

"I do, I'm just impatient."

"Then come on down and let's hit the road," Ethan said.

Mable threw on her favorite crew-neck sweater and a pair of jeans. Then she checked her face and hair in her mirror. Since she wasn't sure where they were going, she threw on some foundation and mascara. After brushing her teeth, she gave herself one last look in the mirror, picked up her bag, and ran down the stairs to start her weekend with Ethan.

Before she could open her door, Ethan had walked around to her side of the car, taken her bag, and put it in the trunk. He opened her door, and she climbed into the seat. She looked over at him as he fastened his seatbelt. Her breath caught. He was so handsome. *But why did it look like he had purple mixed into his brown hair?*

"Did you do something to your hair?"

"What? No, I've been meaning to get a haircut, but I haven't gotten around to it yet." Ethan pulled out of the apartment complex parking lot and headed toward town.

"It looks like there's purple or light gray in your hair?"

Ethan was silent for a moment, his eyes on the road. "I was working on a painting project."

"Oh, okay." Mable looked out the window, "Why are you turning onto Main Street? Don't we need to get on the highway?"

"Nope," Ethan said.

"Huh. Well, now that we're in the car, you can tell me where we are going."

"Nope."

Mable frowned, then pouted, "Please, Ethan, I hate suspense!"

They passed Donnie's Books and Breads, and then Kate's Pupcakes and Clawssants. Mable crossed her arms, resigned to waiting.

At the next crosswalk, Ethan put on his blinker. He drove around to the back of New Age Stones and Witch Crafts.

"Is Hannah in on this?"

"Not really," Ethan said.

"Why are we stopping here?"

"You'll see." Ethan smiled like the Sphinx. He put the car in park and got out. He came around to her side of the car.

She rolled down the window. "Are you just picking something up?"

"No! C'mon, follow me!"

Mable stomped out of the car.

Ethan just took her hand and laughed. She swung their arms, happy that he knew she was only putting on a little act, pretending she was grumpy.

He opened the door to the back stairs of the building and then pivoted away from the back entrance to Zaina's store and unlocked the door to the stairs.

"What the…?" Mable said.

Ethan chuckled and started walking up the stairs.

"Not going to lie. I'm really enjoying this view. You've been doing your squats, and it shows."

Ethan shook his ass and Mable reached up and gave him a love swat.

"More of that please," he said and continued to the second floor. At the second-floor landing, Ethan stopped in front of a door with a simple vine wreath decorated with silk sunflowers.

"Sunflowers! Those are my favorite flowers."

"I know," Ethan said.

He unlocked the door and turned the knob.

"What's going on?" She narrowed her eyes and paused at the door.

His brown eyes sparkled like the last rays of sunlight on autumn leaves. He pulled her hand, "Come in, come in."

Mable looked around the living room. On the far wall was a banner that read, "Welcome Home!" and underneath was a hand-lettered sign that looked suspiciously like it had been made by a couple of kindergarteners. It said, "Mable" and had a stick figure of a person with long blond hair and a triangle skirt.

Mable gasped. "Ethan?" She bit her lip. Could this be what she thought? Her stomach filled with butterflies.

Ethan smiled and took both her hands. "Remember back during the summer, how you told me you were so excited to be alone for the first time in your life at Sean and Nicole's?"

Mable rolled her eyes. "And then Iggy turned out to need a village to raise her."

Ethan rocked his hand back and forth. "So that didn't work out like you wanted, and it got me thinking, how could I help you finally have your own space?"

Mable's eyes started to blur.

"I've watched you at your apartment, and I see how you consider nothing except your room as a place to relax. You don't even have a drawer in the bathroom or a shelf in the fridge."

Mable nodded, "and the walls are paper thin."

"Trust me, I can live my whole life without hearing Carolyn and her girlfriend getting it on again."

Mable wiped a tear from her eyes. "But I can't afford this apartment."

Ethan put his finger under Mable's chin and tilted her head up. "That's the best part." He took her hand and led her over to the kitchen table. On the table was a pile of papers and a pen.

"Here, sit down." Ethan pulled out a chair, and Mable sat down. Ethan sat next to her and pointed at the paper. "Both our names are on the lease."

"But you live at the Belmonts."

Ethan took her hand, "I'll be over at the Belmonts most weeknights, and you'll have the apartment to yourself. Finally, you'll have your own place, but you won't be on your own."

Mable's mouth fell open. "I don't know what to say. Are you sure you want to sign a lease with me?"

"I would love nothing more than being obligated to pay half the rent for the next year with an option to renew."

Mable rubbed her hand against Ethan's thick stubble. "I love you, Ethan. You give me what I need, and you don't demand anything in return."

He turned his head and kissed her palm. The soft feel of his lips against her palm made warmth spread low in her belly.

"Should we christen our new apartment?" she said.

"As soon as you sign the paper, making it official, I'm going to carry you to your new bedroom."

Mable picked up the pen and signed her name with a flourish. As soon as she set down the pen, Ethan scooped her up and carried her to the bedroom he'd finished painting earlier. He carried Mable over to the bed and dropped her onto it. Mable grabbed Ethan's shirt and pulled him down onto the bed.

"Don't you want to see what the room looks like first? Let me get the remote to turn the light on."

"Later," Mable said, and she pulled Ethan down on top of her. She loved having the solid weight of him on top of her. She ran her hands through his hair as he began kissing her neck. He pulled her sweater to the side and kissed the sensitive skin in the hollow of her neck. He sucked lightly, and she let her nails massage his neck.

He came up for air, his stubble scraping along her collarbone. "Take off your shirt," he said.

"You too."

He leaned back on his haunches and pulled off his long-sleeved henley. She pushed herself up, and he helped her get out of her sweater. Underneath, all she had on was a barely there camisole. Her nipples pebbled as he looked at her as if he were ready to devour her.

"I just want to eat you up," he said as if he could read her mind.

"Well, go on then," she said and pulled off her camisole. Mable leaned back on her elbows, and he crawled forward, dipping down to take her left nipple into his mouth. He sucked on her hardened nub, and she moaned. She palmed her other breast, rolling the aching bud between her thumb and forefinger.

Ethan continued to lave her breast and with his other hand, he reached down and cupped her.

"Ethan," she gasped as he pressed against her wet pussy. She needed her jeans off now.

"Take off your pants, baby. I need to taste you."

Mable didn't say another word. She lay back against the comforter, which she was looking forward to getting a good look at later. Quickly she unzipped and pushed down her jeans. She couldn't wait to have Ethan's tongue tasting her, so she slid down her panties with the pants and Ethan was quick to help her finish getting her clothes off. Mable felt the chenille of the comforter beneath her, and it just added to the delicious sensations of the moment.

Ethan pushed her knees apart. She shivered in anticipation as he slowly ran his hands down her inner thighs. When he reached the v of her legs, he used his middle finger to trace her folds, covering himself in her juices. Then, as she watched, he licked her off his finger. She reached down and began rubbing her clit. He watched her touch herself.

There was just enough moonlight coming into the bedroom through the blinds so that she could see the naked need in his eyes as she pushed one of her fingers into her swollen pussy.

Mable smiled and slowly licked her lips while arching her back. She was playing a game, trying to see how long he could hold out before he dove between her legs and began lapping her juices. She needed his tongue on her clit. Just as she was about to beg him, he groaned and put her leg over his shoulder, giving him more access to her pink pussy. She thought of that first time he'd called her pussy perfect, and that, along with his tongue swirling around her clit, almost put her over the edge.

Mable ground against Ethan's face, thrilling in the roughness of his beard between her thighs. He slowly pushed one of his fingers into her warm depths, drawing it slowly in and out in time with his tongue, and now she was bucking against him. He picked up his motion and added another finger. She was so close now.

"Baby!" she shouted, "Yes! I'm so close, I need you!"

"What do you want, Mabs?"

"I need your cock," she said.

Ethan moved away from Mable. She shivered from the sudden lack of contact. He stood up and quickly removed his jeans and boxer briefs. He sat on the edge of the bed and pulled open the nightstand drawer. Mable raised an eyebrow as Ethan took out a condom and ripped it open.

"What? I was a Boy Scout."

"I could not be happier that you are always prepared. Now get back over here."

Ethan rolled the condom down over his gloriously big cock. "Turn over," he said.

Mable got on all fours, her legs spread and ready for him to finish her and himself off. He stood on the side of the bed and pulled her to him. He rubbed himself against her opening and used his thumb to massage her clit. She rocked against him. "Ba-by," she begged.

"I'm here for you," he said, and he slowly pushed down into her, inch by inch, and she made her pussy muscles contract around the length of him again and again until he was deep inside her.

She moaned his name. She knew that even a small sigh from her drove him wild. Her knees scraped against the chenille comforter, and that just added to the overload of sensory stimulation as Ethan slammed into her. His fingers found her clit and within seconds she was soaring. "Baby!" she shouted, and she knew that was Ethan's undoing. He fucked her furiously on their new bed. "Yes, baby, yes!" she said as they came as one.

He draped himself over her as they slowly came down from their high. Her legs trembled, and he pulled out. She rolled over and watched as he hustled off to take care of the condom. Ethan came back holding a soft rose-colored terrycloth robe and an ice cream bar. She put on the robe and took the ice cream bar from him. "You are truly the best." She took a bite of the ice cream bar and then put her hand out, offering him a bite. Ethan took a bite of the ice cream.

"It's oat milk," he said.

"It's delicious."

Ethan sat down on the bed next to Mable and wrapped his arm around her. "The fridge is fully stocked with all your faves and plenty of comfort foods."

"What did I do to deserve you?"

"I have the same question for you."

"You really are the best thing to happen to me, Ethan."

"I can't help but think of a chestnut-colored furball who might say she was the best thing to happen to you."

"You know, if we ever get married, Iggy is going to have to be my maid of honor."

"When we get married," Ethan said.

"When?"

"Baby, I'd marry you tomorrow if that's what you wanted," he said, his eyes brimming with love for her and only her.

Mable threw her arms around Ethan. "Iggy was right. You are the man for me!"

"Is that a yes?"

Mable kissed his cheek. "It's a you better be ready for the day I decide it's time to tie the knot!"

He squeezed her tight and answered, "Anytime, baby, anytime!"

***

Want to know what happens when Susan moves back to Marley Creek and meets Donnie? Read *It App-ened Last Night* https://a.co/d/0gKWIKu0

About the Author

♥

Victoria's love of writing began in grade school, where she won an award for a Mother's Day essay. She spent the better part of her childhood with her head in a book. In high school, she wrote love stories for her friends in which they'd meet their favorite bands or the movie star they had a crush on. Suffice it to say, Victoria was writing fan fiction before fan fiction was a thing. After spending many years starting and stopping writing in various genres, Victoria returned to her high school roots and began writing romance.

Victoria Hamel lives in the Chicago area with her husband, three college-age kids and Bowie the dog. She has run three marathons and based on that experience; she feels qualified to say that reviewing her manuscript for errors was a more arduous task than literally running a marathon. She is a member of the Chicago North Romance Writers Group as well as Contemporary Romance Writers. When she isn't writing, Victoria volunteers for local democrat candidates, watches K-Dramas, or can be found blogging on her blog *First of All...*

You can find the other books in the Marley Creek Romance series here or via any independent bookstore:

https://www.amazon.com/stores/author/B0CSBGDRFQ

Subscribe to my newsletter for exclusive bonus scenes, ARC opportunities, and all the news!